Praise for Judy Fitzwater's previous book, *Dying to Get Published*

"Enjoyable reading for writers hoping to break into the mystery field."
—*Ellery Queen's Mystery Magazine*

"In a roller coaster of hilarity, Fitzwater has crafted three-dimensional characters with warmth, realism, and wickedness."
—*The Snooper*

"Fitzwater provides an entertaining (and for aspiring writers, frustratingly familiar) look at the world of writing and publishing."
—*Publishers Weekly*

By Judy Fitzwater
Published by Ballantine Books:

DYING TO GET PUBLISHED
DYING TO GET EVEN

Books published by The Ballantine Publishing Group
are available at quantity discounts on bulk purchases
for premium, educational, fund-raising, and special
sales use. For details, please call 1-800-733-3000.

DYING TO GET EVEN

Judy Fitzwater

FAWCETT CREST • NEW YORK

A Fawcett Crest Book
Published by The Ballantine Publishing Group
Copyright © 1999 by Judy Fitzwater

All rights reserved under International and Pan-American Copyright Conventions. Published in the United States by The Ballantine Publishing Group, a division of Random House, Inc., New York, and simultaneously in Canada by Random House of Canada Limited, Toronto.

www.randomhouse.com/BB/

Library of Congress Catalog Card Number: 98-96539

ISBN 0-449-00386-8

Printed in Canada

First Edition: February 1999

10 9 8 7 6 5 4 3 2

For Miellyn and Anastasia,
who bring me such joy

I am indebted to many people for their kind assistance: my husband and daughters, who are at the forefront of my efforts; my wonderful editor, Joe Blades, and his outstanding assistant, Malinda Lo; the incredibly talented writers of my critique group: Robyn Amos, Barbara Cummings, Ann Kline, Vicki Singer, Karen Smith, and Catherine Anderson; Nick Protos for his expertise on the restaurant business; and Bob Bockting and Matt Perriens, who lent the manuscript a final critical eye.

Chapter 1

As she perched on the witness stand, Jennifer Marsh steeled herself, her long, taffy-brown hair wound into a neat, businesslike French twist. She might be facing one of the most difficult situations in her almost thirty years on this earth, but she knew exactly what to do, exactly what Maxie Malone, the confident heroine of her mystery novels, would do. She would make it tough for the district attorney and his team, who were determined to put her dear friend in prison for life—or worse. They'd have to force information out of her if they were going to get it at all.

The judge, the prosecutors, and the defense team had been in a sidebar for what seemed like forever—at least five minutes. Why was it taking so long? What could they be talking about? Why didn't they just admit defeat, excuse her, and release her from that horrible witness box?

She looked out over the sterile, upholstered sleekness of the new courtroom. Not a vacant seat in sight.

The only ingredients missing were low ceiling fans, the cloying smoke of cigars, white suits on the defense team, and maybe a statue of a Confederate hero. And those uncomfortable wooden benches and slat-backed chairs. Broad-brimmed hats on the ladies, a hankie or two . . .

1

Okay. So there was a lot missing, not the least of which was a little real justice. Atlanta could do better.

And where was the emotion, for Heaven's sake? A woman was fighting for her life. Yet there sat the spectators, chatting, smiling, passing the time as if they were at a cocktail party or the racetrack.

Where was the heat? Where was the sweat? Where was the smell of fear? And where were those wonderful little paper hand fans that Southerners fluttered in all those vintage movies to indicate their excitement and their despair?

In the middle of the very last row of benches, Jennifer could see her writers' group: Leigh Ann, Teri, April—young, aspiring authors all. Even Monique had come. Of course, she wasn't holding any part of the banner that stretched from Leigh Ann to Teri across April's bulging, pregnant stomach, the banner that proclaimed HANG IN THERE, JEN, the banner that the police officer was even now removing from their grasp.

Her eyes wandered to the row reserved for the press and to Sam—sweet, sensitive, infuriating Sam, who just might turn out to be the love of her life if their relationship ever actually made it to love. He sat there with his fellow journalists, pen and paper ready to represent the *Macon Telegraph.* Sam Culpepper would do his best, bless his heart, but he had a most irritating habit of including *all* the facts in his stories, facts that might be misconstrued by the public. Facts that would point straight to the accused.

Next to him, Jennifer recognized Teague McAfee, cub reporter for the *Atlanta Eye,* the tabloid that daily redefined yellow journalism. Teague had been dogging her trail ever since the murder, and his smug expression ensured he'd do a number on this trial. He loved the seamier side of life and saw it as his mission to expose it, to toss it like fodder to the unimaginative masses. Most likely, he'd toss them Jennifer, too.

In front of the press sat Lisa Walker, grieving widow of the deceased, and a walking stereotype of the blonde bimbo. Red, pouty lips lay below an ample nose and heavily lined eyelids fringed with false eyelashes weeping mascara. Her black suit was cut in a low V, and Jennifer wanted to lean forward and offer her a little advice. *They meant for you to wear a shell under that jacket.* But why bother? Her answer, no doubt, would be "I know."

She tore her gaze from Lisa's tear-streaked face to look at the defense table. Bile gathered in her throat. Dear Mrs. Walker—the *first* Mrs. Walker—her white hair framing her angelic face like a halo, her tiny body swallowed by a padded chair, stared back at her wistfully, expectantly. Brave, surprising Mrs. Walker. If she *had* killed her former husband, no doubt he deserved it. After all, Jennifer trusted Mrs. Walker's judgment. Too bad Fulton County, Georgia, didn't.

The guards passed a hand signal, and Jennifer watched as one of them slipped through the back doors. She caught a glimpse of the crowd teeming like bacteria in the hall outside. A low rumble traveled across the room and reverberated back again. Something was finally happening.

The judge sat up straight, repositioned the microphone, and motioned the lawyers back to their places. Jennifer felt her blood race through her veins at breakneck speed, a flush filling her cheeks.

The Honorable T. S. Leonard shook his head as the defense lawyer's mouth opened. "I've heard all the arguments I intend to consider, and I have my ruling. The prosecution will be allowed to treat Miss Marsh as a hostile witness."

He turned to Jennifer. "That means the prosecution may ask you leading questions that require only a yes or no answer."

Jennifer opened her mouth, but the judge again shook his head. "Only yes or no. I hope I need not remind you again that invoking the Fifth Amendment is a privilege reserved only for people who could be accused of having committed a crime, not for someone reluctant to give testimony. Miss Marsh, you are still under oath."

He didn't need to remind her. That had been the problem from the beginning. Jennifer had sworn on the Bible. To God. She couldn't lie. She'd been reared a good Baptist girl. God would never forgive her, or, at least, never forget. But how could she forgive herself if it were her testimony that sent that wonderful little woman to her execution?

The judge was speaking. "You may proceed." He nodded to the prosecution.

Arlene Jacobs stood. She was short, painfully thin, and dressed in an expensive, beige linen suit. She looked like she hadn't fed for some time, and Jennifer was about to become her dinner.

Ms. Jacobs smiled a wicked, triumphant smile. "All right. Now, Ms. Marsh. Shall we try this again? Did you or did you not, on the night of the murder, travel to Edgar Walker's estate and come upon the defendant, Mrs. Emma Walker, in proximity to Edgar Walker's deceased body, holding a bloody knife that was later determined to be the murder weapon?"

Jennifer closed her eyes and swallowed hard. Even Maxie Malone couldn't get out of this one. There was nothing left to do except answer the question. "Yes," she said, "I did, but—"

Chapter 2

Sam was not happy, and he was making no effort to hide it. Jennifer noted an unnatural clench to his jaw as he glanced in the side mirror of the Honda and threw his hands up at the car in front of them before blending with the traffic traveling south on I-75 toward Macon.

He hadn't said a word to her since they'd left the courthouse, and that was just fine. She didn't want to talk to him either. If it weren't for Jaimie, she would have given up men long ago. Of course, it didn't help that every time she got close to Sam her biological clock started bonging like Big Ben.

Her hand found the flat of her stomach. Jaimie, her unborn child, was impatient for a father, and Sam was a prime candidate for the job. But until Jennifer proved herself as a mystery writer and until she was absolutely, utterly, and completely certain that Sam was the one, Jaimie would have to remain an unfertilized egg. Fatherhood was not reversible. Once those chromosomes were joined, there would be no going back, no returning them to Kmart for defective parts or unpleasant characteristics like spurts of insensitivity. No, Jaimie would simply have to wait until she was sure, sure she was ready for marriage, and sure Sam was the right man.

Normally, he had all sorts of qualities to recommend him, but he did have his moods—like now—when he could be totally unsympathetic.

On the witness stand, she'd had to say what she did. It was the right thing to do. Justice was worth fighting for regardless of the consequences, and if he couldn't understand—

"I had to go to three different ATM machines before I found one that would take my card," Sam said.

Interesting that he could talk at all with all that tension in his face. She'd prefer to ignore him, but she couldn't. As much as she hated to admit it, she owed him big time. She could be spending the night in jail.

"It's only two hundred dollars," Jennifer offered in the most saccharine voice she could manage. "I'll pay you back next week."

Money. It was always getting in the way. Why, they wouldn't even let people have food without it.

"I've got a catering job with Dee Dee next Wednesday. That should cover it."

At least Sam got a regular paycheck. She had to rely on the social calendar of Macon's elite for her money, that and the little she got from the trust fund from her mom and dad's estate. And the pittance in royalties she split with Sam for their nonfiction book, *The Channel 14 Murders*.

Being an unpublished mystery writer was expensive— all those stamps, not to mention reams and reams of paper, writers' conferences, long distance calls, boxes and boxes of tissues for when those rejections came in, as well as—

"Contempt of court, Jennifer. The judge explained to you as simply as he could. You were to answer yes or no, nothing else. And what was all that nonsense about freedom of speech you were spouting as they led you out?"

Jennifer sighed. She knew exactly how a court of law worked—at least how it was *supposed* to work. She had watched *all* the *Perry Mason* reruns. She'd even written a marvelous courtroom scene in her Maxie Malone sequel, and there was no Arlene Jacobs standing up to squelch Maxie's brilliant revelation.

"Okay, so I'm a little behind on Georgia law."

"Georgia?"

"All right, then, law. Are you satisfied?" She slumped back against the upholstery of the Honda.

Sam had that infuriating fixation on accuracy. Must be part of his journalistic training. That's why she preferred writing fiction. She could create any characters she wanted. And she would have deleted Arlene Jacobs—before she'd had a chance to object to her testimony. Where was her sense of sisterhood, anyway? The woman's pores leaked testosterone.

It was going to be a long ride back to Macon, eighty miles, and she had no desire to spend it carping at Sam. He was a good guy, and not bad-looking, especially when he combed back his dark hair and a few strands escaped to fall over his right eye. And those eyes. They were the deepest, darkest blue.

She shook her head. It was best not to concentrate on Sam's good points when he was angry with her. After all, he had a few faults of his own—like his complete lack of empathy. She might go down for defending Mrs. Walker, but she would do so with her dying breath. That sweet little woman had practically saved her life when she had been accused of murder, and there was no way she would abandon Mrs. Walker now.

Jennifer turned and stared out the car window, the lush green of kudzu whizzing past her, and thought, if only she'd ignored that phone call from Mae Belle in the wee hours of that terrible Monday morning. If only she had insisted that Mae Belle go back to bed and leave her alone . . . .

Jennifer shook her head. Mae Belle had been worried, really worried. And she had been, too. She shuddered and tried to remember, hoping somehow to dredge up something from the events of the past several months that might help her piece together what really happened that night, the night Edgar Walker got himself killed.

It had been close to three in the morning when the telephone had rung, waking her from a sound sleep and setting Muffy, her greyhound, off on one of her frantic back and forth fits around the apartment.

Jennifer didn't function well in the middle of the night, never had, and she was in the midst of one of those cock-eyed dreams that, in her woozy state, seemed like a great plot for a novel. It left her trying to remember the story, which had something to do with a hermit, a swamp, poisoned mushrooms, and a siren that went off at regular intervals—undoubtedly a bestseller—as she groped for the phone.

"What?" she croaked into the receiver.

Breathless gasps came across the wire.

"You've got the wrong number. That would be 1-900-GET-LOST."

Jennifer started to hang up when she heard a dainty voice squeak out, "Please, dear. Please, this is Mae Belle, Emmie Walker's friend. I'm afraid something's happened to her. You're the only one I could think of at the moment who has a car, you see, and well . . ." The pause was so long, Jennifer thought Mae Belle might have passed out, or worse yet, passed away. The woman had to be close to eighty.

She sat up in bed and pulled the phone into her lap. "Mae Belle," she demanded, "are you there?"

"She left a little before midnight, you see, and said she'd be straight back, no later than one-thirty. And here it is three. It can't be good, not good at all."

Jennifer shook the last bits of her dream from her mind, pushed Muffy down from the side of the bed where the dog was licking her kneecaps, and let what Mae Belle was trying to say penetrate her consciousness. Something had happened to Mrs. Walker.

"Where did she go?" Jennifer asked.

"To the estate, of course."

Of course. "*What* estate?" Jennifer's mind was not functioning sufficiently well to draw conclusions, especially from facts not in record.

"Her husband Edgar's, just south of the city."

If she remembered correctly, the Walkers had divorced years ago and were not on the most amicable terms. "What is she doing there?"

"Oh, my. I'm not quite sure. The last time it was to turn the water in the swimming pool a rather lurid red, and the time before that had something to do with chickens, but I don't exactly know what—"

"Are you saying Mrs. Walker was playing *pranks*?" Jennifer asked.

"That's such a juvenile word, now isn't it? No, I think Emmie would prefer to say she was putting a little interest into Edgar's rather dull existence."

How thoughtful of her.

Jennifer rubbed her face briskly with the palm of her

hand. She had a feeling she wouldn't be going back to bed anytime soon.

"And you called *me* because . . ."

"Someone must go see, I'm afraid, and none of us here have a way out there. You could hardly expect us to go by bus, now could you?"

When, exactly, had Jennifer's expectations come into play here? Besides, she was a staunch supporter of public transportation.

"How did Mrs. Walker get there?"

"She has a special arrangement with a taxi service. She supplies them with a beeper for when she's ready to be picked up. I called them, but I'm afraid they claimed she never beeped." A sob came across the line, followed by a throat clearing and a distant voice saying something about "buck up."

"We're just asking that you cruise by, dear," Mae Belle continued, "to see if Emmie is waiting beside the road."

"We?"

"Jessie's with me, of course. She sends her love."

She would. Jessie was the epitome of a finely aged Southern belle, Scarlett O'Hara with white hair.

"You do realize I'm in Macon, in Macon sleeping, and it *is* three in the morning."

"Of course. It's not that far from you. I'll give you directions. It couldn't take you more than, say, half an hour or so."

Chapter 3

Or so translated to an hour and fifteen minutes.

Old Edgar had done pretty well for himself as proprietor of the Down Home Grill restaurant chain. Not only could he afford to keep ex-Emmie in the luxurious comfort of O'Hara's Tara, one of Atlanta's most exclusive condominiums, but he had grounds, guarded by a high fence, that ran on for an indecent length of road.

Jennifer pulled her little Volkswagen Beetle off to the side of the pavement near the large gate, stopped the engine, took up a flashlight and got out. Pole lights illuminated the area.

What could Mrs. Walker possibly be up to this time? Jennifer looked around. No sign of her. She'd hoped to find her friend waiting to be rescued, the beeper in one hand and a handful of dead batteries in the other. Why was life never that simple?

Jennifer cocked her head and listened. Everything seemed quiet except for some overzealous crickets. She felt incredibly ridiculous lurking around some man's estate in the middle of the night, especially when Mrs. Walker was probably already home and sipping tea by now. Mrs. Walker had demonstrated more than once that she was far more resourceful than most people half her age.

Even so, a shiver of unease scurried across the back of Jennifer's neck. Maybe Mrs. Walker hadn't made it home. Maybe she was still out there somewhere in the darkness.

Jennifer flashed the light across the cast-iron, spearlike rails of the fence. If her friend was making regular visits to the place as Mae Belle had suggested, there had to be a way in. Mrs. Walker might be spry, but she couldn't scale that kind of fence any more than Jennifer could, not at her age and diminutive height. No, there had to be an opening, and most likely it'd be marked in some way. She worked her way down the fence.

As she was about to give up, Jennifer found something about sixty feet from the gate, near a wild plum tree. Two of the metal spears hung loose at the bottom. It made a space barely big enough for a child, let alone an adult, to slip through. Fortunately, Jennifer was still in her skinny, writing-through-dinner mode—her full attention focused on her new Maxie Malone adventure. This one would make three, all as yet unpublished, all waiting patiently for some agent to discover and launch an unbelievably successful and lucrative series.

Maxie was everything Jennifer wasn't. She was shrewd, clever, a master of disguises and voices, and she'd never, ever get stuck halfway through a fence like Jennifer had now. She sucked in her stomach and dragged her hips the rest of the way through the narrow opening, scraping her calves in the process.

She rolled onto the grass. Someone had definitely been through here before, and more than once. The grass was flat and no weeds grew at that spot.

Jennifer regained her balance and, momentarily, her common sense. What did she think she was doing—besides breaking and entering? And with her luck, ol'

Edgar probably had a pack of people-eating dogs roaming the grounds ready to make a midnight snack out of her.

Jennifer loved dogs, but anything over waist high—Muffy excepted—made her nervous, and at five-six, her waist was fairly high. Fortunately, she had grabbed a bag of Muffy's treats and stuffed them into her jeans pocket on her way out of the apartment. She hoped Dobermans and Rottweilers were as fond of Snausages as greyhounds were.

The moon was high and almost full, casting a creamy glow over the grass and leaves. Jennifer cut back up toward the gate and the driveway, following the asphalt for a brisk five minutes before catching her breath in amazement. Even in the dim light, the house was glorious. All white, all columns. It stood shimmering in the dew of the evening, the outside lights only hinting at its magnificence. Wow! Had Mrs. Walker lived here, or had Mr. Very Successful Edgar Walker acquired this property after he had *un*acquired Mrs. Walker?

Jennifer closed her mouth and turned her attention back to the business at hand.

Everything out front looked normal. No evidence of foul play on the lawn or the porch. But where the heck was Emmie? Something wasn't right. Everything was too quiet, and Jennifer's fears were taking on a life of their own.

Mae Belle had mentioned something about the pool—that had to be around back. She didn't know what Mrs. Walker had done with the chickens, and she didn't want to know.

She followed a stone path around the house into the radiance of a softly lit patio and a huge, kidney-shaped swimming pool lined with underwater lights.

Jennifer blinked. She could make out some kind of dark

blob in the water on the far side of the pool. Another dark blob lay near it on the pool's concrete apron. A breeze must be stirring because the on-land blob seemed to be aflutter.

Jennifer gulped. Blobs were not her thing—not in the water and not on land. She much preferred monsters with a definite shape to them. Something with a front and a back so she knew which direction to run in.

Courage—she had to have some inside her somewhere, if only she could find it. What would Maxie Malone do? Investigate, of course. Curses. Did she have to live up to her own creation? She drew herself up. If Maxie could do this, so could she. She shone her flashlight across the pool, the fractured light shimmering off the surface of the water, and inched forward. There were no such things as monsters, no such things. So why were her hands shaking and her knees threatening to buckle?

Near the pool edge, her foot must have tripped some kind of infrared sensor because a loud wail blared and an array of lights flooded the pool.

Jennifer froze in terror as the blob in the water turned into a body floating facedown. It looked big and bulky, too massive to be Mrs. Walker, and it appeared to be dressed in a sports jacket, the back of which was floating eerily on top of the water.

A moan drew Jennifer's attention to the other blob, which seemed to be trying to sit up. As it did, Jennifer thought she detected a familiar curve to the diminutive shoulders and the silver curls escaping from a knit cap.

"Mrs. Walker?" Jennifer offered tentatively over the siren. The dark figure turned in her direction. "Thank God," she declared. "I was beginning to think I'd never find you, and then if I did—"

"Jennifer?" the figure asked. "Oh, dear. Is that you? You should be at home in bed."

At least they were in agreement on that point.

As Mrs. Walker turned back, she seemed distracted by something in her lap. Jennifer watched in horror as Mrs. Walker grasped an object and then held it up in the light. It looked like a knife with at least a nine-inch blade, though something was somehow preventing the blade from shining.

"Don't move another inch." The words were measured and threatening. Jennifer stopped and turned to see an amply endowed woman in a lacy negligee, standing on the steps leading down from the house. Her bleached blonde hair lay loose about her shoulders, and she held a double-barrel shotgun straight out in front of her. "Take one more step, and you'll be picking buckshot out of places you didn't even know you had."

Chapter 4

Watching dawn break through a police station window was not Jennifer's favorite way to spend the morning. As a matter of fact, she couldn't remember the last time she saw the sun come up, preferring that it be firmly and securely in its place in the sky before she started her day.

Unfortunately, her day had started some time ago, and her immediate concern was the growth of her rap sheet. Unless some miracle happened, it was about to receive another entry.

Detective Frank Sweeney had raised his eyebrows at her when the police brought her and Mrs. Walker into the station house. He made some rude remark under his breath about hoping never to see her again after her last arrest and then left after the briefest of interviews. Then he must have forgotten all about her because she'd been sitting on a bench outside his office, hugging her knees, and waiting for the last forty-five minutes.

She was tired, it was close to six-thirty in the morning, and she hadn't had a bite to eat since yesterday at noon. Except for that doughnut between chapters around four P.M. and, close to midnight, that bowl of ice cream—strawberry cheesecake. Not her favorite, but definitely Muffy's. All of which was beside the point. She was hungry, and the police had better feed her. She had a constitutional right to food while in their care, and they had to honor it or—

"You can go," a gruff voice said.

Jennifer twisted to see Sweeney's burly body standing behind her. He had on another one of those cheap gray suits. Must get a quantity discount.

"What?" she asked.

"You heard me. Your story checked out. Now get yourself out of here."

"What about Mrs. Walker?"

"She's being booked."

"For?"

"And don't go anywhere. The D.A. will want to talk to you. They'll be calling you as a witness."

"I am not!" she declared.

"You saw the knife; you saw Emma Walker holding it."

"But she didn't do it," Jennifer insisted.

Sweeney gave her one of those smiles from the nose down. His eyes remained cold steel. "Go home." He started out the door.

"But I've *got* to help her," she called after him.

He stopped and turned, his eyes softer this time. "Are you religious?" he asked.

She nodded, a cold chill spreading through her bones.

"Then pray. That's about all anybody can do for Emma Walker."

Prayer was good, and she definitely intended to indulge in a healthy dose, but she knew that God never worked alone. He helped those who helped themselves. If Sweeney's estimate of the situation was correct, Emma Walker was going to need lots of help. God's *and* Jennifer's.

* * *

The nightmare just kept getting worse. Mrs. Walker was in jail, Jennifer was the main witness against her, and some idiot had parked in her space at her apartment building. She'd driven all the way back to Macon only to be irritated like this? And the lot wasn't even half full.

Jennifer pulled into a visitor's slot, jerked the notepad from between the seats, and scribbled down the license number of the little green Hyundai that, for some reason, looked vaguely familiar. She'd march straight to the apartment manager's office and insist that the owner be found immediately. She slammed the car door, turned, and stopped short.

Teague McAfee was sitting on the top step leading up to her building, looking at her, an impish grin on his face. He was cute in a thin, overly energetic, early twenties kind of way, his brown hair cut short on the sides, long and loose over his forehead. He wore a buttoned-down shirt and jeans and looked a whole lot better than she did at the moment.

"Hey, Marsh. 'Bout time you got home," he called.

Something inside of Jennifer squirmed. The guy must have connections at the police department—paid ones, most likely. Edgar Walker was hardly cold in the morgue, and the hungriest cub at the *Atlanta Eye* had already heard about the murder, gotten himself down to Macon from Atlanta, and staked out her place. Quite a feat for a cold-blooded animal so early in the morning.

Jennifer realized she could have spun on her heel and skedaddled, but McAfee was standing between her and her coffeepot. And she knew if she fled, he'd be there when she came back, whatever time that was. He was like that. Tenacious. Like a pit bull. What's more, it was only eight in the morning. Where would she go? The mall didn't open till ten.

She crossed the lot and started up the stairs.

He stretched his long leg across her path. "How's tricks?"

The twerp. She'd taken him out for lunch once to do some research on a book, and now he wanted to treat her like they were old friends. After forty-five minutes of listening to the stunts he pulled to get information better left unknown to anybody anywhere, let alone printed in a newspaper, she had politely excused herself, paid the check, and offered him the name of an exorcist.

Still, he had called her. Said they were "fellow writers." Was she the only one who noticed they had nothing in common? She was five years older than he was, and his writing, if she could call it that, had nothing whatsoever to do with hers.

"Crawled out from under your rock to feed off the dead?" she asked, stepping over his leg and continuing up the stairs.

Immediately he was on his feet, keeping pace as she jogged, with the last ounce of energy in her body, up the inside stairs to the second floor. No way she was getting caught in an elevator with him. She stopped in front of her door, and he slipped between her and the lock.

"Look, all I want is five minutes of your time. That's all. I promise. You won't even have to sleep with me." Then he laughed as if he thought that was funny. It was.

She'd give him five minutes all right. She slipped her door key between her second and third fingers. One good, strategically placed jab . . .

"Hey, look, I was joking, Jen. Lighten up, will ya? I've

got a whole file on this Walker character. He's big business in the Atlanta area. Why'd the old broad knock him off?"

"Someone pays you to do this?"

He nodded. "Good money. I hear you know this Emma Walker personally. If you want to do her a favor, tell her to talk to me, give me her sob story. The paper will play it up big, and we'll get the public on her side. 'Spurned Wife Exacts Justice on Slimy Ex.' I get a story; she gets two to five."

"And me?"

He pursed his lips and pretended to think for a moment. "You get the satisfaction of knowing you did the right thing."

She was surprised he knew the words "the right thing." She wouldn't have thought they were in his vocabulary, at least not in that particular sequence.

"Move," she growled.

"What say I buy you some breakfast?"

"What say you don't?" She knocked loudly on the door, and Muffy went into a barking frenzy that made her sound truly ferocious.

McAfee backed up, and Jennifer slipped the key in the lock. "Like to come in and meet my dog? She hasn't been fed this morning."

He took a card out of his pocket and handed it to her. "Maybe this isn't the best time. But you'll call me before all of this is over."

Jennifer watched as he walked back down the hall. She hoped she'd never be so desperate that she'd have to call on the likes of Teague McAfee.

Chapter 5

Jennifer turned the key in the lock of her apartment as she saw Teague McAfee slither into the elevator. She pitied the poor wretch he'd track down next. But that was none of her concern. She was home where she could lock her doors, draw her shades, turn off her phone, and collapse without interference.

Cautiously, she swung open the door and braced for Muffy's welcoming onslaught.

Muffy was the only one in the world who loved her truly and completely. Unconditionally. Actually, the dog did have a few requirements for her affection, like on-time feedings, at least two walks a day, and some generous rubbing about the ears and neck. Whatever. With Muffy, she had achieved a near-perfect relationship. The dog was faithful, loyal, forgiving—and strangely absent. She'd been there not two minutes ago, barking as if she would rip through the door and tear McAfee into little pieces. It wasn't like her to abandon a good fight.

"Muff?" she called tentatively.

The blinds were drawn tight, leaving the modest living room/dining area in a shading of gray.

"You here, babe?"

She heard a whimper in the direction of her worn-out

sofa. She flipped the light switch, and her heart jumped. Sam was slouched in a chair, his legs stretched out in front of him and crossed at the ankles, his tie loosened, his sleeves rolled up, his fingers steepled and resting on his lips. He was staring gravely back at her.

Muffy, planted at his feet, gave out a puff of air, shook her head, and dropped it onto her paws.

"How did you . . ." Jennifer began, then was suddenly aware of her tattered sweatshirt and stained jeans. Her hand went to her hair. The early morning dew had left little ringlets along her hairline and anywhere a strand had escaped the knot at the back of her neck. And she hadn't bothered with makeup at three in the morning. She must look just like she felt. That was one scary thought.

Sam dropped his hands into his lap. "Mrs. Ramon, across the hall, let me in. I took a chance that you'd leave a key with a neighbor. Found her on the second try."

"She's not supposed to—"

"Hey, the dog had to be fed and walked." He sat up, and Muffy found his hand with her head. *His* hand. Whose dog did she think she was anyway?

"You did that?" she asked.

"Somebody has to look after you two girls."

She found that statement both endearing and infuriating at the same time, like so many things about Sam. "We can take care of ourselves very nicely, thank you."

"Taught Muffy to let herself out, have you?"

Sam never seemed to know when to leave anything alone. She tossed her keys on a table by the door and went toward the small nook of a kitchen. She needed coffee. *Now.*

As she reached for the carafe, she realized that it was full and the little red light of the machine was on. Who did he think he was, waltzing into her house, fawning over her neglected dog, and making her the coffee she so desperately needed?

She poured a cup and took it—black—back into the living room, collapsing onto the sofa and savoring one long soothing slug of the bitter, hot liquid.

"Okay, you've saved me with coffee and rescued Muffy. We're fine. You can go now."

She didn't mean to seem so ungrateful, but she didn't trust Sam's motives. When she first met him, he'd practically swept her off her feet, but that was *before* she found out he'd been wooing her to get her help with a story. And now the question was what price tag came with the coffee. It might be more than she was willing to pay.

"How's Emma?" he asked.

Hah! She knew it. She slapped her mug down on the coffee table, almost spilling its contents. Dang if she'd drink the stuff now.

"I'm not uttering a word." She jutted out her chin.

He pursed his lips and shook his head at her. And then he was next to her, pulling her against him, and she was too tired to pretend she didn't need him. The tears started, and she was making a terrible mess of his shirt.

"They think she did it," she blubbered into his chest. "They think Emma killed her ex-husband."

He stroked the tears from her cheek. "Did you see her at the police station?"

She shook her head against his shoulder and sobbed. "They took us down in separate cars." Then she drew back, suddenly dry-eyed. "You're not taking notes, are you?"

"Of course not."

"But you *are* writing the article for the newspaper."

"I understand you're a witness."

She sat up straight, swiping at her eyes, grabbed up her mug, and blew hard on her coffee. "Nope. Didn't see a thing."

Gently, he guided her chin toward him so she couldn't avoid his eyes. "I know Emma didn't kill anybody. I'm on your side—yours and Emma's. You know that."

She did know it, but she also realized he had a job to do, and he would do it with honesty and integrity. And to any honest person—herself included—darned if it didn't look like Emma did it.

"Did you see anybody else at the estate?"

"This is all off record?" She tugged away from his hand.

"Of course."

"Besides Emma, I didn't see anybody except for some blonde who pointed a shotgun at me."

He let out a puff of breath, obviously irritated with her lack of faith in him—that and probably the fact she had nothing to tell him. "That would be Lisa Walker, Edgar's current wife."

"So I gathered. What do you know about her?"

"Not much. She's younger than he was by a good forty years, give or take a birthday or four."

"A gold digger," Jennifer declared.

"Maybe, but the couple of times I saw them together, she was pretty touchy-feely."

"You saw them together?"

"Sure. For the paper. The Down Home Grills are a growing business."

"The way she was swinging that shotgun around, she didn't look much fond of anyone."

"How'd she react to Edgar's body?"

"Now that did look genuine. Once she got close enough

to the pool to realize what had happened, she covered her mouth with one hand and fell sobbing to her knees. But she never once let go of that gun."

"Who called the police?"

"Must have been part of the security system, because they were there in no time flat."

"Is it true Emma broke into the estate?"

Hah! There it was, that journalistic phrase: *Is it true?* He wasn't getting another word out of her. "I don't know and if I did, I wouldn't tell you." She crossed her arms and leaned smugly back against the sofa.

Sam looked gravely at her. "Maybe you're right. I don't think I want to know."

He stood up, grabbed his sports jacket and briefcase, then bent to give her a quick peck on the lips. "I'll call you later."

He was all the way to the door before she managed two syllables: "Thanks, Sam."

He nodded, and then he was gone, leaving her with a half cup of lukewarm coffee and a terrible feeling in the pit of her stomach.

It was one thing to be frightened herself. It was quite another to see that same fear reflected in the eyes of someone she'd expected to assure her that everything was going to be all right.

Chapter 6

"You look awful," Leigh Ann declared, getting right up in Jennifer's face and staring at her with jade green eyes, her dark, chin-length hair cupped behind each tiny ear. "You do know that, don't you?"

Of course she knew it. She had mirrors in her house. She even looked in one occasionally. Not everyone could be a sexy, sultry vixen like the heroines Leigh Ann wrote in her romance novels. They could make it through a five-page sob session without a single mascara streak, not to mention a puffy eyelid or a lipstick smear.

Jennifer squirmed away from Leigh Ann and scooted closer to Teri on the floor, her back leaning against Monique's sectional sofa. She should have stayed home tonight—she had only been released by the police that morning—but attending her writing group's Monday night sessions was almost an obsession. She never missed one. Writing was her focus, her beacon, her link to sanity. And right now it would be nice if her critique partners would cut her a little slack. They were her friends, closer than sisters. Only sometimes they acted a little too much like sisters.

"You been in some kind of fight?" Teri asked, examining Jennifer with her big, brown eyes in that deceptively sweet cocoa face. "You look pitiful with those huge circles sagging at your cheeks."

Now even Teri was turning on her. She'd like to see what Teri looked like after being up half the night, sneaking onto an estate to find a murdered man, being dragged down to the police station, fending off some crazed tabloid reporter, and then coping with Sam.

Monique took in an audible gasp of exasperated breath, and everyone paused. As irritating as Monique could be, she did keep an iron hand on the group—being older and, Monique thought, wiser than the rest of them. Not to mention published, even if it was only one book. "Let's get back to the business at hand. April was telling us about a new book she has in the works when you came in, Jennifer."

"Could be an iron deficiency," April suggested, munching on a piece of peanut-butter-stuffed celery and staring straight at Jennifer's face. She patted her rounded belly. It seemed like April was perpetually pregnant. "I have to take pills for that. This little guy gobbles up every nutrient I take in."

Looked like there might be one or two calories left over padding out April's rosy cheeks and arms.

"Your *book*," Monique reminded April from her rocking chair throne.

"Well, you all know I've been working on the Whacky the Duck adventures, but the market for picture books is really tight right now and there are so many ducks out there. I mean, it's hard to make Whacky stand out from the flock. Anyway, I thought why not go for something really, really different, like a bat!"

"Does a witch go with that bat?" Teri asked, folding her long bronze legs into a lotus position.

"Of course not. This is a good bat." April tugged defensively on one of her blonde curls.

"I don't know about that. Anything that produces guano . . ." Leigh Ann said.

"Let April tell us her proposal. You all know better than to interrupt," Monique declared.

April cleared her throat. "Barney Bat is not your stereotypical flying mammal. He *is* nocturnal. I didn't think I could change that even for artistic purposes, but he does come out during the day. It's on one of those day outings that he runs into four-year-old Billy, who, of course, at first thinks he's rabid. They team up, and I thought I might make it a mystery series. So whatcha think, Jennifer? I realize the plot might be a wee complicated for the preschool set, but what's the fun in writing fiction if we can't push our limits now and then?"

Poor April. She never quite got the respect she deserved, and this crazy picture-book mystery series wasn't helping. How could she tell April to trash the whole stupid idea without demeaning her talent or crushing her creative spirit? Jennifer was too tired to devise a tactful comment, and her mother had always taught her, "If you can't say something good about someone, don't say anything at all." So she decided to pass the buck to Leigh Ann. "What do *you* think?"

"I don't feel qualified to respond. Romance is my area." Leigh Ann took in a seductive-sounding breath and looked over at April. "Now if you have Barney meet up with Bettina Bat, then maybe I could give you a few ideas. You've got that deep, dark cave to work with, and sonar. Sonar's very sexy. Sending off throbbing signals into the steamy darkness, never knowing where they'll wind up . . ."

Why had Jennifer thought talking to Leigh Ann would help? Her version of Barney Bat's adventures would have an NC-17 warning label plastered across the cover.

Jennifer turned to Teri. Surely, Teri would save her. She wrote romantic suspense. "And you?"

"I'm still lost in that pulsating cave with Leigh Ann."

"Jennifer. *You're* the mystery writer," Monique demanded.

She'd have to bite the bullet and answer. "I think preschoolers are a little young for mystery stories. What if you bump the kid's age up to eight or so and try for an early reader? And you might use another mammal, one that's more cuddly, one with fur. Maybe a flying squirrel. It worked for Bullwinkle."

April looked startled, as if the peanut butter in the celery had bonded her teeth together. She tapped the last bit of the stalk against her cheek. "You know, maybe I could. Thank you, Jennifer."

Monique turned her powerful, smug expression in Jennifer's direction. In her haste to get to the meeting, Jennifer had walked out the door without the latest pages of Maxie Malone's newest adventure.

Well, she had an adventure of her own going on, one that could definitely use a little editing. They'd hear all about it later—probably already had on the news. Only they didn't know that she was involved, which was just as well. Or that Mrs. Walker was *her* Mrs. Walker. It was best not to confuse this group with facts. While their minds worked well in fiction mode, real life was quite another matter.

"Did you bring something to read?" Monique asked.

"No. I've got an idea for brainstorming. You know that guy I killed off in chapter one?"

"Rock on," Teri said, lifting her feet off her thighs and twisting at the waist. "I loved it. Industrial espionage. Drowned in a vat of chocolate syrup." She licked her lips. "What a way to go."

"You can keep the drowning part, but let's make it a swimming pool, and add a knife wound through the heart."

"A swimming pool filled with chocolate?" Leigh Ann asked.

Jennifer sighed. Why was she doing this? "Make it water."

Teri stared at her indignantly. "Water? You're trading in chocolate syrup for water?"

"Okay. Leave the syrup, I don't care. But the guy's now well into his seventies, married to his second, much younger wife. So who killed him?"

"Wife number one, of course," Leigh Ann offered.

"No, it wasn't," Jennifer insisted.

"Always is," Leigh Ann declared from her place on the sofa. She picked up one of the throw pillows and batted it at Jennifer's head.

"I'm writing this," Jennifer reminded Leigh Ann as she disarmed her. "And I say it wasn't the first wife."

"Good alibi, huh?" Teri concluded.

"No alibi, but she didn't do it."

"Better work on that alibi, or you'll never get the police to believe it was someone else," April offered. "But maybe that's what you want. It's the first wife who hires Maxie Malone, right?"

Jennifer nodded. If only Mrs. Walker *could* hire Maxie Malone. If only she could be as brilliant as her own creation. Suddenly a strange, crazy idea came over her.

Maybe in some weird, mixed-up kind of way, Mrs. Walker could hire Maxie Malone. Maybe . . .

"Yeah," Jennifer said, wondering for a moment if she'd completely lost her mind. "She hires Maxie Malone."

Chapter 7

Rufus Donaldson's body bobbed in the open vat like a chunk of unmelted baker's chocolate. Some murderous swine had devised a most apropos end to the candy mogul's life—swallowed by his own sweet obsession. Maxie could hardly take her eyes from the scene. All she could think was what a waste of good cocoa.

The police would be there any minute, but Maxie had something more important on her mind at the moment. She had found Donaldson while making her security rounds of the factory. She would have missed him entirely if she hadn't heard the moaning coming from the grid just above the tank. She'd hauled herself up the treacherous scaffolding only to find Emily Donaldson dazed and half out of her mind. And now she was trying to make the older woman comfortable until help arrived.

A sudden movement caught Maxie's eye. They weren't alone.

"Make any sudden moves, and you'll be picking buckshot out of places you didn't even know you had."

The voice came from somewhere below. Slowly, Maxie raised her hands and turned to stare straight into both barrels of a shotgun.

It was Lorelei Donaldson, Rufus's second and much younger wife.

Maxie practically laughed in the bimbo's face. "We'll see who's picking what out of whom," she declared.

What kind of dialogue was that? The kind that could get Maxie killed. Jennifer blocked out the last sentence and deleted it.

Maxie silently searched the woman's face. What was Lorelei Donaldson doing at the factory?

Good question. She'd figure that one out later.

Lorelei might have won this round, but the match wasn't over. Once the police arrived and confirmed Maxie was in Donaldson's employ . . .

Jennifer hung her head. She'd already gotten that far in real life. *Just let it flow, Jennifer*, she told herself. She took a deep breath, sat up straight, and let her fingers find the keyboard.

. . .Maxie would turn Atlanta upside down if she had to to find out who wanted Rufus Donaldson dead. And she knew exactly where to start . . .

Muffy nuzzled her head under Jennifer's elbow.

Rufus's Chocolate Heaven.

"Of course. That's it," Jennifer told Muffy, pushing back from the computer and giving the dog a much appreciated scratch behind her ears. "I'll call Mrs. Walker, find out what I can about Edgar's restaurants, and then do a little snooping."

Woof! Muffy barked her approval, of either the scratching or the plan. It was hard to tell which.

Jennifer grabbed the phone and punched in Mrs. Walker's number. Surely she'd been released by now, Tuesday morning.

Someone answered on the first ring. "Mrs. Emma

Walker's residence. Mrs. Walker is not accepting calls at this time, if you would like—"

"Mae Belle, it's Jennifer."

"Jennifer. Oh, thank God. We tried to reach you last night, but no one answered. I had no idea when I called you that—"

"It's all right, Mae Belle. Is Mrs. Walker there?"

"Certainly, dear. But she's so distraught over what happened, I'm not sure now is a good time."

No doubt Mrs. Walker had *some* feeling for her ex-husband. They had to have been married for a good while.

"I'm sure it will take some time for her to adjust to the fact that Edgar's dead," Jennifer began.

"No," Mae Belle said. "It's Tiger."

Tiger was Mrs. Walker's pet. Most likely he was a mutated Chihuahua, although Jennifer still wasn't convinced he could be classified as canine.

"Tiger?" Jennifer offered, visualizing the ugly little creature with its ragged potato chip ears sticking out from a head the size of an orange, and black, beady, unearthly eyes that hid an unhealthy obsession with leather.

"They've had to rush him to the hospital, I'm afraid. Jessie was feeding and watering him, of course, but Emmie was gone for so long, he must have thought she'd abandoned him. When the police released her and she finally got home, she discovered him prostrate on the floor in some kind of respiratory distress."

Sure he was. Tiger probably waited until he heard the key turn in the lock and then threw himself gasping onto the floor. That wretched creature was *not* to be trusted. She'd had dealings with him before.

"He's being kept overnight for observation."

They'd better watch him closely. Jennifer suspected he

changed forms in the dark. "I'm sure he'll be fine. He's a hardy little fellow. Now, do you think I might speak with Mrs. Walker?"

"I'll see, dear."

She could hear murmurings in the background. Sounded like Mrs. Walker had a houseful.

"Jennifer, how very thoughtful of you to call." Mrs. Walker's voice was strong and steady—a good sign.

"How are you holding up?"

"Well enough. I'd find this all quite interesting if I didn't have this irritating murder charge to contend with. It was, after all, simply a matter of time."

"What?"

"My dear, you can't screw everyone you come in contact with and not eventually get screwed yourself. Oh my, I don't mean that literally."

Jennifer hoped not. She'd seen Edgar's Down Home Grill commercials on TV. Not a pretty sight. Her least favorite had Edgar sporting a cowboy hat and standing next to a plaster of paris bull, holding a noose around the monstrosity's neck and a cup of Edgar's Special Steak Sauce in his other hand. She'd thought the first time she saw it (and before she realized he was Emmie's ex) that the man should be shot on principle. Of course, she had to admit that being a vegetarian might color her response. Still, if her reaction was anywhere near typical, the suspect pool for Edgar's murder could extend to the entire Atlanta viewing area.

But maybe Mrs. Walker had someone more specific in mind. "Who do you think did it?"

"If I were going to make a list, I'd certainly put my own name at the top, but as I know I didn't—not that I haven't thought about it—we'll have to go on from there, won't we?"

If worse came to worst, Mrs. Walker could plead insanity. Jennifer cleared her throat. "Is there a number two on that list?"

"I'm sure that at one time or other the thought must have crossed the minds of most of his business associates, staff, suppliers. Perhaps an old school chum. Fortunately, we had no children or they'd be up there, too, I should think."

If Mrs. Walker's assessment were correct, Edgar must have come across nicer on the tube than in real life— which meant *nobody* liked him. Jennifer sighed. People could have been standing in line to off Edgar Walker. The question was who got to him first.

"Actually, I'm probably giving you entirely the wrong impression of Edgar. It wasn't that he was malicious. He was simply careless—careless with those he loved, careless with those he didn't. I've often thought carelessness should be the Eighth Deadly Sin. Don't you agree?"

She did. It was far easier to deal with people who hurt others intentionally than those who never gave a passing thought to the destruction they caused.

"Where did Edgar spend most of his time?" Jennifer asked.

"At the original restaurant, not too far from his home. That was his main office. He had managers for all of the others. Kept them in line more by phone than in person, I understand, but he did drop in occasionally."

Just as she (and Maxie) had suspected. "Do you think I might go by the restaurant?"

"That's a wonderful idea, Jennifer," Mrs. Walker gushed. "Infiltrate. I'll see that you get a position there."

"No, really . . ." Jennifer hadn't realized Mrs. Walker had any influence over the actual operation of the restaurant.

"Now don't be silly. It'll only be for a week or two, however long you need to get the lowdown on Edgar's situation. Why don't you drop by the restaurant, shall we say, about four Friday afternoon? That should give me time to make the arrangements."

Jennifer didn't have a catering job scheduled with Dee Dee that weekend anyway. And working at the restaurant might be the easiest way to get a feel for the business. She could waitress or hostess for a few hours, blend in with the scenery, keep her ears open. She just hoped she wouldn't wind up bussing tables or washing dishes. "Okay, I'll give it a try."

She might even hear some gossip about Lisa. After the first wife, the most likely suspect had to be the second. It might help to have some idea where she fit into all of this.

"Do you think it's possible Lisa stabbed Edgar?" Blunt, but how else was she going to ask it?

"Oh, dear, I suppose so. They had a prenup. But a will is quite another matter, isn't it? She will be a far wealthier widow than she would be a divorcée. But she won't get all the restaurants, if that's what you're thinking. I own the controlling share, dear. After all, it was Daddy's money."

Chapter 8

Great! Mrs. Walker had plenty of motive for Edgar Walker's death. She despised the man, and if her lawyers wound up letting her testify, Jennifer felt sure she'd tell the jury exactly how she felt. It was good Jennifer didn't live in Fulton County. She'd hate to be called for jury duty on this one.

She pulled her little powder-blue Volkswagen into the parking lot of the original Down Home Grill, cut the engine, and turned to look at the restaurant facade. It was even tackier than it appeared on TV. How could any self-respecting person work in a place decked out like that? The walls were a turquoise stucco creating a bizarre mingling of Mexican and Floridian styles. Turquoise and pink striped awnings shaded the large windows and were echoed in pink and white stripes directly under the clay-tiled roof. And there, near the door, was that hideous plaster of paris bull that costarred in Edgar's commercials.

It was only four o'clock in the afternoon, and the parking lot was already half full. Not bad for so early in the afternoon, even on a Friday. So the food had to be good, if animal flesh charred barbarously over an open fire could be good. Obviously, Edgar's patrons did not share her dietary preferences. Tofu would, after all, fall right through those little slits on a grill.

Jennifer had thrown on a mid-calf, sleeveless cotton dress and a pair of sandals for the trip to Atlanta. It was hot, her Bug had no air-conditioning, and she could almost feel stray strands of hair contracting into ringlets around the clip that held the hair off her neck.

By contrast, the inside of the restaurant was icy cold. Central Georgia was having one of those weeks of late spring when the temperatures topped ninety-five degrees and gave an early taste of what August would bring. Walking from that kind of heat into a refrigerator was enough to stop the stoutest heart. Jennifer settled for a good shiver.

At least the place was pleasantly bright, sunlight from the large windows bouncing off cream-colored stucco walls. Strains of country music twanged in the background.

A perky young woman dressed in cowboy boots and a mid-thigh sundress greeted her, a menu in one hand. "Edgar Walker's Down Home Grill welcomes you to the home of the Eddie."

"The Eddie?"

"Thin strips of succulent sirloin, batter-dipped and deep fried, served with Edgar's Special Steak Sauce. One?" She looked around Jennifer as if expecting a busload to follow.

"No, thank you. I'm here about a job."

"Oh," the girl said, stuffing the menu back under the podium. "We've had three girls quit." The girl leaned in confidentially. "The owner got himself murdered, if you didn't know."

"Really?" Jennifer put on her best surprised look.

"Yep. Fortunately, it wasn't here. I don't go in for that

blood and guts stuff. If I walked into, say, the kitchen and found somebody's insides all over the floor—well, I don't think I'd be comfortable working here anymore."

Jennifer nodded sympathetically. People did have to have some standards.

"Our new manager hasn't come in yet, so you really should be speaking with Mrs. Walker, but she stepped out about five minutes ago. And I don't know when she'll be back."

Lisa? Lisa was at the restaurant—and hiring the help? Somehow Jennifer had suspected she would be engaged in loftier pursuits—like painting her toenails.

The girl was nodding. "Yep, and boy was she mad. Got some call from her lawyer's office and took off like a bolt of lightning."

For someone who toted a shotgun, mad was not a good thing. Now might be a good time for her to leave, but the hostess wasn't about to let her escape.

"We really are shorthanded. We're only half full and the wait staff is already hopping. We've had to give them extra tables, and in two hours this place is going to be nuts."

A young couple, each carrying a child under the age of three, came in, the wife toting a diaper bag bigger than her baby. Never too young to introduce those little fellows to the joys of red meat.

The hostess leaned over and whispered into Jennifer's ear. "You have a seat while I get these folks settled, and then I'll get Roy to help you."

If Lisa just left, Jennifer should be safe for at least, say, an hour. She could risk a quick conversation with this Roy, whoever he was.

The girl repeated her spiel and led the family off, a booster seat under one arm, a high chair trailing behind her.

Jennifer sighed and sat down on a bench where patrons waited when the place was really full. Too bad Edgar didn't have one of those health food boutiques. She wouldn't mind serving cappuccino and bran muffins. In fact, she could be enjoying a flavored coffee right now instead of fighting off the smell of seared beef.

A screech of tires drew Jennifer's attention to the parking lot. A black Jag stopped directly in front of the door, and Lisa emerged, hair flying, in black leather vest and miniskirt, sunglasses covering most of her face. She slammed the door of the car with such force the front glass of the restaurant rattled.

"Here comes Mrs. Walker now," the hostess offered, returning to her station. "She must have forgotten something."

At least Lisa looked unarmed. Jennifer put on her best just-ignore-me-I'm-part-of-the-scenery face and scooted back toward a large fern.

Lisa tore into the restaurant and pulled the shades from her face. Jennifer watched as the hostess seemed to shrink in height before her very eyes.

"Where the hell is—"

Lisa stopped cold, turned and stared at Jennifer. For a moment she looked shaken. Was that a spark of fear she detected in Lisa's eyes? In an instant it was gone, the firm set of her jaw back in place. "You won't get away with this," Lisa said, each word a distinct threat.

Get away with what? She hadn't even ordered a salad.

Lisa turned back to the hostess. "Did you find a manila folder anywhere around here?"

The girl nodded and extracted something from under

the podium. "I'm sorry. I didn't realize it was yours. I thought one of the guests—"

Lisa jerked it from her and faced Jennifer, her ample chest heaving with anger. "My lawyer is going to get this straightened out. You are not coming in here and taking over. I won't have it, do you hear me, Jennifer Marsh?"

With that, Lisa left, her Jag spewing gravel.

Jennifer sat stunned, feeling like she'd been slapped in the face, her cheeks every bit as red. Maybe this would be a good time to leave. She stood, her legs a little shaky, and shouldered her bag.

The hostess's face was as red as her own. "You said you were here about a job. Do I feel stupid!" The girl slapped her forehead. "Why didn't you give me your name or at least tell me you were our new manager?" Smiling shyly, the girl extended her hand. "Welcome aboard, Ms. Marsh. We've been waiting for you."

New manager? Jennifer reached for the girl's hand, more to steady herself than anything else.

This was all Emma's doing. Didn't she know infiltration, as she so aptly put it, had a sense of subtlety to it? Beheading the king and taking his place was *not* infiltration.

"We got the word not half an hour ago you'd be coming in. My name's Suzy. I usually work five to eleven, but Louise was out today so I'm in early. I'll tell Roy you're here."

Jennifer should have made a run for it, but her reflexes weren't working right, and before she could bolt out the door, a hulking man, maybe mid-thirties, with closely shorn dark hair, wearing a white, short-sleeved shirt open at the throat, was standing over her. He looked like someone she'd like to have on her side in a fight. His manner seemed cautious, and she could tell he was sizing her up.

He was talking but she missed the first part of his sentence, waiting for the ringing in her ears to subside.

" . . . so why don't you follow me? I'll help you get settled in. Your office is back this way." At least his words were friendly enough.

Like a robot, she trailed after him. What else was she going to do?

He led her into the kitchen. "Grill's over there." He pointed at a huge, open pit with enormous vent fans hanging above it in the center of the room. Steaks of every shape, size, and kind were sizzling over coals, and an aroma as thick as Texas perfumed the air. A short man with Latin good looks in a white hat and jacket was hovering nearby.

"That's Gus, the best chef in the state."

If that were true, Jennifer wondered, why was he wasting his time on steak?

Gus stared at her curiously, and then said, *"Buenas tardes, señorita."*

But Roy didn't pause for introductions. "He doesn't speak much English," he explained. "Your fry baskets are over there." He pointed to the right. "And your salad area is near the refrigeration unit, the potato and vegetable fixin's on the far side."

"Vegetables?" Jennifer asked hopefully.

"Well, vegetable of the day—fried okra. Tomorrow it's corn."

Variety. No wonder the place was so popular.

They swept on through a glass-paneled swinging door in the back. "And here's your office." Roy opened the door and let her in.

It was not at all what Jennifer had envisioned. It was small, windowless, with a cheap metal desk, file cabinets, and that utilitarian shelving usually reserved for garages or basements. And it was a mess.

"We start serving at eleven, stop at eleven with a cook crew of six and a wait staff of seven, 'cept we've lost three waitresses with the fuss over the murder," Roy said. "Leaves us a bit shorthanded."

"So Suzy was telling me."

"Well, I guess that's about it." He turned to leave and then turned back. "I almost forgot. You'll be needing these." He handed her a ring of keys.

"Roy," Jennifer said, taking them and tucking them into her pocket, "I don't know anything about the restaurant business."

He smiled, she hoped at her candor but most likely at the foolishness of the situation. "Never stopped them from hiring anyone before." He looked her up and down. "Seems you've got the usual qualifications."

Jennifer's cheeks burned.

Roy stared at her briefly, as though light were dawning somewhere in that massive head of his. "At least the qualifications Mr. Walker usually looked for in his staff."

He'd left her an opening, and if she were lucky, it'd be just enough. "Like I said, I know nothing about the restaurant business. I'm here because . . ." *Maxie, why the heck am I here?* Could she trust Roy? Did she dare? She could almost hear Maxie sigh at her ineptitude.

"Actually, I'm an efficiency expert hired by Emma Walker," Jennifer rushed on. "She thought it best I come in under the guise of a manager. I won't be here long. I'm to assess the situation, the current staffing and future needs, ultimately recommend a new manager." Nothing like throwing a bone to a harried employee. Besides, it wasn't exactly a lie. It was quite possible she would influence the ultimate staffing needs. "But I'd rather the rest of the staff not know why I'm really here. It'll make my work a lot easier."

"Special consultants, efficiency experts." Roy shook his head. "Look, I've been working here for the last seven years. I know everything there is to know about it, and this place runs like a charm. It's very simple really. We cook good food and we serve it."

And if she had anything to do with it, the restaurant would continue to hum along as it always had. She had no intentions of upsetting the harmony of Edgar's Down Home Grill. And she certainly wouldn't dream of depriving the patrons of their carnivorous cravings. As long as Roy was around, she felt sure they would remain well-fed. "But you're not the manager?"

"Mr. Walker kept that title for himself."

"Assistant manager?"

He nodded, a smile playing about his mouth. Why didn't he care about the title if he was doing most of the work?

"If I'm hearing you right, *you* were the one overseeing what goes on here."

"About sixty hours a week worth. Every day except Wednesdays."

"With all that experience, why didn't you leave?"

Again he grinned at her. "You'll figure it out soon enough."

"And Lisa?" Even as the words escaped her mouth, Jennifer realized what a risk she was taking by asking.

"What about her?" Roy seemed a little wary.

"Is she around much?"

"More than I am."

"Really." So Lisa took more than a passing interest in

the restaurant's operation. "And how do you like working with her?"

Roy shrugged. "She's tough, but she's fair. She doesn't ask anybody to do anything she wouldn't do herself. Anything else?"

So Lisa had at least one supporter. Jennifer shook her head.

And with that he left, pulling the door shut behind him.

Jennifer made her way to the desk, pulled out the swivel chair and collapsed into it. She only had a short amount of time. Lisa would be back, and when she got there, she'd come straight after her.

Chapter 9

"Okay, I'm looking for three T-bones, four sirloins, and a filet mignon, all overdue. What are you doing? Strolling out to pasture to round up cattle? Try looking in the fridge. Let's move it, move it, move it!" Jennifer snapped her fingers for emphasis, just like her mother used to do. Man, how she'd hated that. Silently, she promised Jaimie she would never snap her fingers at her/him when she/he was born. She balled her hand into a fist to keep herself from doing it again.

"People are starving out here." She clamped her other hand over her mouth, in an attempt to squelch the urge to say even more. She didn't know what had come over her. All that power. She'd only been at the restaurant a few hours, and already she felt like she was king of the mountain.

And the amount of meat now gracing the grill was unimaginable. It was like witnessing deforestation, only this was cattle, not trees. And she could only stare at it, like a really bad car crash.

A platter filled with a huge, sizzling steak and a baked potato bigger than her fist whizzed by her at the warming bar. One of the waitresses picked it up before it came to rest and took off for the dining room.

"We've got a complaint at booth seventeen. Want I should get Roy?" Suzy asked from behind her.

Jennifer shook her head. "Roy's busy helping Gus. I'll handle it. Just point me in the right direction."

Booth 17 was nestled next to the fish tank and was occupied by a distinguished-looking man with gray hair wearing a suit and tie, dining alone. A piece of steak hung from the end of the fork he had poised over his plate.

"Does this look like medium rare to you?" he asked before Jennifer even had an opportunity to introduce herself. It'd been some time since Jennifer had tasted steak, let alone inspected it, but this piece was definitely oozing red with a telltale area of pink.

"I can see that piece is underdone. I'll be glad to—"

He looked at her as if she'd lost her mind. "This is medium. I ordered medium *rare*." The man dropped the fork with a clank. "Get me a new steak. And make sure you leave some life in it this time."

"Don't you watch *60 Minutes* or *20/20*? Haven't you heard about the hazards of eating undercooked animal flesh, not to mention—"

"Mr. Arnett, good to have you back, sir." Roy reached around her, offering the man his hand and nudging Jennifer away. "Let me get that out of your way. One of the waiters must have picked up the wrong order. I'll see that you get an Eddie sent out right away with our compliments while we get another steak grilled for you. By the way, Miss Marsh, you have an urgent telephone call."

Who could be calling her at the restaurant? No one knew she was coming to Atlanta, no one except, that is, Mrs. Walker. She swung through the kitchen, scooping up a bowl of okra on her way. Once in the office, she picked up the phone and punched line one, which was blinking red.

"Jennifer Marsh," she said, popping a fried morsel into her mouth.

"How's it going?" Mrs. Walker's sweet voice floated across the line. Johnny Mathis was singing "Chances Are"—loudly—in the background.

On occasion Mrs. Walker suffered from a bit of paranoia. Fortunately it was nothing that a bit of overblown music to defeat any potential listening devices couldn't cure. Usually she preferred Wagner. At least Johnny was easier on the ears.

"Why didn't you tell me you intended to make me the manager?" Jennifer asked, trying to control her anger.

"Oh, that. It never pays to start at the bottom. Besides, I wanted to get you access to the files. You *have* had a chance to look through them?"

"I was doing that when they called me out to help. This place is unbelievable. We've got them waiting in a line down the porch."

"Of course you do, dear. They come for the Eddie and for Edgar's Special Steak Sauce. Have you tried it yet?"

Jennifer had grabbed a baked potato about five-thirty and dabbed on a bit of sauce, just for a taste. She'd wound up burying the spud in its creamy goodness. "It's delicious. What's in it?" she asked, chomping on some more okra.

"It's a secret, of course. Edgar never would tell me. I think he was scared to death someone might get hold of it and bottle it."

"Like you?"

"Well, of course, dear. Do see what you can find in those files. Who knows when we'll have an opportunity to have at them again. Roy will take care of everything out front. He's quite efficient."

"So he told me."

"Actually, I called to ask you to stop by, if you have time, before you head back to Macon this evening. I know how hectic it can get there, but try to be here at least by nine if you possibly can."

Jennifer hadn't yet recovered from their Monday morning adventure. But she couldn't turn down Mrs. Walker.

"I'll be there."

Jennifer hadn't even hung up the receiver when the door burst open. She blinked hard. For a second Lisa looked like some kind of superhero—back-lighted, hair flying, tough as nails—standing there in the doorway with the anger of the righteous, ready to fight injustice.

Unfortunately, Jennifer had a terrible feeling she was on the wrong side of this fight.

She sucked in air and took a better look at her adversary. Actually, Lisa looked more like a biker chick. Even less reassuring. And there was only one way in and out of that office, and Lisa was standing smack in the middle of it.

Jennifer stood, pulling her purse onto her shoulder, and edged along the back side of the desk.

"Out!" Lisa roared.

Whatever was left in those files could not be worth bodily injury, at least not Jennifer's. Besides, she *was* the interloper here. "I'm going, I'm going," she whispered soothingly, inching toward the door.

When Jennifer got within a yard of her, Lisa blocked her path. "I want you to take a message back to Emma."

Jennifer prayed it was a verbal message, nothing like a human ear or, heaven forbid, a horse's head.

"You tell her I built this restaurant over the last ten years, regardless of whose money started it, and I don't intend to give up control of it. Got that?"

"Loud and clear."

Lisa stepped aside, and Jennifer scurried past her.

"I won't let her have it," Lisa called after her. "No matter what!"

Chapter 10

When Jennifer got to Mrs. Walker's condo at O'Hara's Tara, she was still reeling from her encounter with Lisa. That girl had muscles, not to mention one major attitude.

Shakily, she pressed the doorbell. Tones of "Georgia" sounded over Johnny's mellow tenor, which was now on to "The Twelfth of Never." Jennifer could only hope that CD hadn't been on continuous loop since their phone call.

Mrs. Walker threw open the door and hugged her. A faint growl heralded the arrival of a small, furless creature that skidded across the entryway, threw himself at Jennifer's shoe, and attached himself like a tiny octopus about her foot. Mrs. Walker seemed totally oblivious to the unruly behavior of her dog.

"Come right in, dear. We've been engaged in some work of our own."

"Tiger," Jennifer managed to squeak out.

"Yes, dear. He's *so* glad to see you."

Jennifer took a step. He was, indeed, firmly affixed—like a tick.

She was having trouble hearing above the music. "What's with Johnny Mathis? I thought you preferred classical."

"Oh, that's Jessie's contribution. She refused to listen to the 1812 Overture again."

Love songs were definitely more Jessie's style, and, Jennifer had to agree, one time through that battle was plenty in one day.

Mrs. Walker led Jennifer—and Tiger—to the plush living area. The floor-to-ceiling windows stretched across the back of the large room and created a breathtaking backdrop of the night lights of Atlanta.

Hunched around the dining table were Mrs. Walker's pals: of course, Mae Belle, with her toothy grin, and a well-rounded Jessie, and three people Jennifer had never seen before—a nice-looking elderly gentleman, and a young man and woman, probably a few years older than herself, who shared a startling appearance.

They were both tall and pale, with blond, almost white hair, his neatly trimmed, hers straight and chin length. They shared the same slim build and narrow shoulders, but the man wore an expensive, custom-made suit, while the woman had donned a free-flowing, ankle-length frock.

Discreetly, Jennifer slipped out of her flats and scooted them—and their cargo—under the table. At least for the moment, Tiger seemed to need them more than she did.

"You know the girls," Mrs. Walker said, "and this is Walter Ornsby."

"Attorney at law, retired," Mr. Ornsby assured her, bowing politely. His hair and mustache were both full, more salt than pepper, and Jennifer wondered if he was what a small-eared Clark Gable would have looked like had he made it to his seventies.

"Walter lives upstairs," Mrs. Walker explained, "but don't let him fool you with that retirement line. He's still my lawyer. Has been for more years than we can both remember.

"And I don't believe you've met the twins, Babs and Benny."

They smiled the same smile with the same lips. It was eerie.

Benny shook Jennifer's hand. "Nice to meet you."

As he let go of her hand, the woman took her turn. "Aunt Emmie has told us—"

"All about you," Benny interrupted. "We're her younger sister's—"

"Alma's children," Babs finished.

It was like watching a Ping-Pong match.

"The twins have been *so* concerned," Mae Belle explained.

Benny looked down, studying his fingernails. "Nasty business."

Babs nodded enthusiastically. "Nasty. Uncle Edgar—" She choked on the name. "We can't believe he's gone." Benny pulled her to him while Jennifer could only stare. It was like hugging a mirror, except for their clothes, of course.

"I told them they should both be at work." Mrs. Walker sighed. "But they've insisted on being here ever since the, uh, occurrence. They simply won't listen to me. Never have. Even when they were the tiniest tots."

"Family comes first," Babs declared. "The restaurants will do—"

"Just fine," Benny said.

"Restaurants?"

"Babs manages the Down Home Grill in Marietta. Benny has the one on Peachtree," Mrs. Walker explained.

Of course. Daddy's money. But Jennifer wondered how

the two could function separately, each being incapable of more than half a sentence.

"And someone else is here, too," Mrs. Walker said just as Sam Culpepper meandered in from the hall and the direction of the powder room.

Jennifer caught her breath. What the heck was he doing here? His articles about Edgar's death for the *Telegraph* had been sympathetic, and he'd managed to include the fact that she was an aspiring novelist. Still, he was first and foremost a member of the press, and therefore, in this particular case, a potential adversary. Why Mrs. Walker would consider involving him—

"Close your mouth, Jennifer, and come over here and help us," Mrs. Walker ordered.

"Help you what?"

Sam came up beside her and squeezed her arm. "Don't panic," he said in her ear. "I'm off duty."

As if a reporter was ever off duty.

"We're planning strategy," Mae Belle explained.

"That is, if there's anything left to plan," Jessie added.

"But I thought you had the best defense team the South has to offer," Jennifer said.

The group exchanged glances. Mr. Ornsby stepped forward. "I'm afraid my learned colleagues—Mr. Larue and Mr. Heckemyer—are of the opinion that Emma should plead guilty."

"Cop a plea?" Jennifer asked, her stomach doing a quick churn.

"Sadly, yes, if you care to put it that way," Mr. Ornsby drawled, his distinguished steel gray eyebrows drawing together in dismay.

"How dare they?" Jennifer demanded.

Babs nodded enthusiastically. "How dare they?"

Benny was nodding, too.

Mrs. Walker shook her head. "I appreciate all of your concern, but they're looking at the evidence. I was seen *holding* the murder weapon. They even have an eyewitness." Jennifer blushed hotly, all too aware of her role as a nail in Mrs. Walker's coffin. "We can hardly expect them to work miracles, now can we?"

For the amount of money Mrs. Walker was shelling out to that duo, a miracle was the least Jennifer expected.

"Mr. Larue and Mr. Heckemyer believe that in view of Mrs. Walker's advanced age and spotless reputation—" Ornsby began.

"And a tendency toward the fanciful," Jessie threw in.

"Ah, yes. Well, in view of all the, ah, factors involved and her most sympathetic appearance," Ornsby continued, "she might be looking at no more than two or three years in prison if we can get the charge reduced to second degree murder."

"You can't be serious," Jennifer choked out. She found a chair and sank into it.

Babs and Benny surrounded her, one on each side. Sam looked on, his hands in his pockets.

"Now don't get yourself into a fret," Mrs. Walker soothed. "We're simply examining options."

Prison was not an option, not for a year or even a few months, at least not as far as Jennifer was concerned. She'd spent most of one day in a cell herself when she was accused of communicating threats, and it was no place for a decent human being like Mrs. Walker. But then, if Emma pleaded not guilty and were convicted without a plea agreement . . . Jennifer couldn't let herself think about that.

Sam found her hand and bent down in front of her. "Don't underestimate Emma," he whispered.

Sam was right. Mrs. Walker was not one to go down without a fight. She straightened. "So what's the plan?"

Mrs. Walker sighed. "I'm afraid I've been relegated to a defensive posture. My attorneys—and Walter is in agreement—have assigned me the task of accumulating all the evidence that would demonstrate how Edgar's death will work to my disadvantage." She raised her eyes to the ceiling, perhaps looking toward a higher power, but most likely to keep from rolling them. "They forbid me to go to the restaurant or have any contact with Lisa or any of Edgar's associates. I'm afraid, dear, I've been hog-tied."

Mrs. Walker looked at Jennifer with big, round eyes. "And I'm afraid you have, too, which is why I asked you to stop by this evening. Mr. Heckemyer called. He received a communication from Lisa's attorney, a friendly chat, as he described it."

Mae Belle humphed. "A threat's more like it."

Mrs. Walker sighed. "In any case, he is of the opinion that you simply can't be appointed acting manager. Benny has volunteered. As a matter of fact, he and Mr. Heckemyer had already discussed it and simply hadn't bothered me with the details. In any case, Mr. Heckemyer doesn't want you down at the restaurant. He says we've already compromised what little objectivity we could have claimed with you as a witness."

Well, she had no desire for another go-round with Lisa. What's more, she'd seen more beef today than she had hoped to see in her lifetime. Still, the situation was worse than she'd let herself imagine. The defense attorneys wanted to cut their losses. But at what ultimate price for

Mrs. Walker? A few months could be a death sentence in and of itself, considering Emma's age.

"My attorneys will conduct a full-fledged investigation, of course," Mrs. Walker continued.

"We've every reason to believe they'll find the culprit and put an end to these horrid accusations," Mae Belle threw in.

Jessie's head bobbed in agreement.

"And exonerate Aunt Emmie," Babs insisted.

The group fell silent as Johnny Mathis continued to croon that love could conquer all. Boy, was he out of touch.

Jennifer stood. It had been a long day, too long, and she'd been exposed to more assaults on her morality than should be permitted in a single twenty-four-hour period. And keeping up with the Doublemint Twins was putting too much of a strain on her tired brain. "I've got to go."

"Once you get home, I want you to forget about this case and get on with your life," Mrs. Walker insisted. "Write that breakthrough novel of yours."

"Sounds like a plan," Jennifer agreed, ducking under the table to retrieve her shoes. She pried Tiger loose, he snapped, and she swatted his nose. She crawled backed out, slipping on the shoes and handing the creature to his owner.

"I think this belongs to you," she said absently.

Mrs. Walker took the wiggling mass, chastised him for being a naughty boy, and held him behind her back as Jennifer bent and kissed her on the cheek. Then Jennifer let herself out the door. Sam was right behind her.

She punched the down button on the gleaming brass elevator, as Sam rested his shoulder against the elevator's frame.

"You can't print any of this," she insisted.

"I don't intend to."

She had been pretty dreadful to him. She hadn't returned either of his last two messages on her machine. They were supposed to be dating, but once Jennifer latched on to something—a new novel or some other obsession, such as who killed Edgar Walker—she instantly developed tunnel vision. Her friends, the few she allowed close to her, had to deal. She didn't mean to be thoughtless, and when he looked at her with those deep, dark soulful eyes like he was doing now, she couldn't quite remember what it was that had been so much more important . . . .

She offered him a crooked smile. "My place, not this coming Friday, but next, say seven o'clock. Pasta all right?"

"Anything you make is fine."

The elevator dinged open. Almost too tired to move, she forced herself inside and punched L. He kissed his fingertips and touched them to her lips. "See you later." Then he turned and sauntered back down the hall.

"Where are you going?" she called after him.

"I've got a few more questions for Emma," he called back over his shoulder.

If it wouldn't have made her look completely foolish, Jennifer would have lunged after him, out of curiosity to know what he wanted to ask Mrs. Walker, and out of her childlike concern that she'd be missing something.

The elevator door thumped in her face. Well, that was fine. She'd had enough time to get through most of the personnel files before Roy pulled her out of the office to help, so she knew a thing or two that Sam didn't. Like the fact that Edgar had hired a young woman as a "special consultant" for fifty grand, although she hadn't had enough time to find out just what kind of consulting she was supposed to do.

And then there was Roy, who was hauling in a cool hundred grand a year as assistant manager. No wonder he didn't care what title he had. If someone would pay her that kind of money, they could call her just about anything they wanted.

If the lawyers didn't want her at the restaurant, it was okay with her. She had a more compelling assignment: find out what made Roy the most expensive assistant manager in the state of Georgia and maybe the whole Southeast.

Chapter 11

So this was what being on a stakeout felt like—dull, boring, and exceedingly uncomfortable. Jennifer squirmed in the front seat of her Volkswagen. Her rear end had gone numb fifteen minutes ago, and still no sign of Roy.

Wednesday was his day off, at least that was what he'd told her. Of course, he did keep late hours, working at a restaurant that didn't close until eleven. Still, he only had one day in the whole week to call his own. Would he really waste it sleeping in?

Actually, that didn't sound like a bad idea, especially after getting up at the crack of dawn to drag herself to Atlanta to find Roy's apartment building. She yawned and glanced at her watch. It was almost eight-thirty. He'd better get a move on, because if he didn't and she didn't find something to do while watching, she was going to fall asleep.

She rummaged in the backseat and pulled out an apricot Danish left over from a breakfast job she'd catered with Dee Dee last week, and chomped it down. It was a little stale and a little gooey, but it was food.

She was licking her fingers when Roy appeared through the front doors of building number nine. She scrunched down as best she could and peered over the dashboard. He

61

was wearing a white T-shirt, sweat pants, and athletic shoes. Not exactly an Adonis, but he looked to be in pretty good shape. He jogged down the steps, back up again, and then down. Oh, great. He must be out for his morning exercise.

He made a full circle of the parking lot, then trotted over to a Ford Bronco, got in, and zipped out before she realized what was happening.

Frantically, she cranked the engine with her sticky fingers, threw it in gear, and puttered after him. As she pulled onto the main street, she could just make out the dark green vehicle turning left at the light at the intersection ahead.

Jennifer rolled down her window, threw out her arm, and waved up and down, forcing her way across two lanes of traffic, horns blaring. Maybe Roy wouldn't notice. He was already out of sight.

She made it to the turn lane as the yellow threatened red. Saying a little prayer, she floored the gas pedal, the engine kicked in, and she zipped across the intersection, her heart in her throat. Tailing suspects sure looked a lot easier in the movies.

They were in a residential area now. Roy had to be taking some sort of shortcut, but to where? She lagged back, letting him wind through the neighborhood, speeding up as best she could whenever he made a turn and left her sight.

As she came around a curve, she saw a four-lane highway directly ahead. The Bronco didn't even pause at the stop sign before turning right. Jennifer's single tap on the brakes allowed a swoosh of traffic to block her path. She gnashed her teeth. She hadn't come all that way and spent all that time to be foiled by Atlanta's rush hour traffic.

Closing her eyes, she scooted out in front of a silver Lexus, not her smartest moment. The Lexus nudged up against her bumper. She glanced in her rearview mirror. The driver was actually shaking his index finger at her. The nerve. He swung up beside her and showed her one of his other fingers.

She kept her eyes on the road and chugged forward, intent on finding the Bronco somewhere up ahead, but the next light caught her. She craned her neck, searching. Where the heck had it gone?

She needed to get her bearings. She knew Atlanta fairly well but had no idea where she was. But as she moved forward, the road suddenly became familiar. The Down Home Grill couldn't be more than a few blocks ahead.

Jennifer spied Roy's Bronco parked next to the Dumpster in the back alley of the restaurant, only a few yards from the kitchen door. She swung onto a side street, parked, and walked back to the Down Home Grill. Wedged into the front pocket of her jeans was a healthy canister of pepper spray. Maxie would, of course, be toting a gun. Roy was one big guy, and she had no idea what role, if any, he might have had in Edgar's death. But Jennifer had a phobia about guns ever since she'd fired one once. Too loud, too much of a kick, and far too scary. If the spray didn't work, maybe she could hit him over the head with the can.

She crept up to the kitchen door, trying to look as nonchalant as possible—the last thing she needed was some nosy neighbor calling the police—and put her ear to the door. It was solid metal.

Maybe she could find something in her purse to jimmy

the door. She pulled it open and rummaged in the bottom. Her hand hit against a bulky ring of keys, the set that Roy himself had given her and she'd forgotten she had. Well, if he hadn't wanted her to use them, he shouldn't have given them to her.

She circled to the front door and searched the gloom through the glass. She could see a light coming from the direction of the kitchen. What the heck was he doing in there?

Carefully, she tried keys until she found one that fit. Poised to run, she turned it and waited. Nothing. No alarm. Roy must not have reset it when he came in. Good. She slipped through the door and into the darkness.

The noise of metal against metal echoed from the kitchen. It mingled with Roy's slurring of the lyrics of some country western tune.

Jennifer slung her purse around her neck, dropped to all fours and scooted across the linoleum of the dining room to the swinging door of the kitchen. She sat back on her heels and listened as Roy twanged a chorus about some pickup truck.

Gently, she pushed up, slowly drawing herself to her full height. Pressing her cheek against the metal support at the warming bar, she allowed one eye a look into the kitchen. Roy was dumping something into a huge bowl that sat on one of the stainless steel counters. An array of containers was set out in front of him as he slopped the mixture with an enormous whisk. Then he filled two containers with the mixture and started a new batch, all the time singing loudly about the new paint job on the truck.

Jennifer slumped back against the door frame for support. So this was where the sauce came from and why Edgar was willing to cough up over a hundred grand a year to an assistant manager. Roy knew the recipe. Edgar must have given it to him. And if Roy came in to make it even on his day off, did that mean nobody else knew it? With Edgar dead, Roy could name his price. He didn't need a restaurant to make a fortune.

With thoughts skipping wildly through her mind, she didn't notice that the singing had trailed off or that the swinging door behind her had silently opened. She turned to slip away and came nose-to-chest with Roy's hulking form, an iron skillet poised directly over her head.

Her breath left her, and for a moment the lightness in her head had her convinced she'd dreamed up his image. But a quick touch of Roy's chest felt far too real. He was as solid as that frying pan.

She felt for the pepper spray wedged in her pocket. Somehow, it seemed woefully inadequate under the circumstances. Besides, her muscles had joined her head in the light department, and her hand wasn't exactly accepting orders.

"I could have killed you," Roy said, lowering the skillet.

She agreed and was most thankful that he hadn't. She grinned up at him, all innocence. "Roy, what are *you* doing here?"

"Me?"

"I stopped by to get something for my report for Mrs. Walker and—"

"Whoa. You aren't supposed to be anywhere near this place. Lisa said—"

"Of course, you're right, but I didn't think anyone would be here," she lied, adding a little prayer to herself that lying to keep from being killed might be viewed as an exception to a pretty adamant rule. "And I really hate to leave things half done, especially when someone's paying me to—"

"Nobody's paying you to do anything." Roy's grip on the skillet tightened. "I know who you are and I know why Emma sent you here."

For two seconds this conversation had seemed to be going so well. "And why would that be?"

"You're after the sauce, like everybody else."

"The sauce?" she repeated, as though she hadn't noticed that there *was* a sauce at the restaurant.

"Don't act like I'm stupid," he warned.

Roy seemed intent on a certain scenario, and she might be better off going along. Besides, sometimes a half truth worked better than an out-and-out lie. "Okay, you caught me. I was following you."

"Following me?" He seemed taken aback.

"I figured out you were the one making the sauce," she fibbed, "and I wanted to talk to you. Alone." Her eyes darted about the darkness as if someone might be lurking in the shadows. Roy followed her gaze. "I want to make you a proposition."

"A proposition?"

This guy would have made a great parrot. "Have you ever considered what that sauce would be worth by itself? Why set your sights on managing a local restaurant when you produce a product that could be on every supermarket shelf in America. I mean we're talking more money than—"

Roy was shaking his head.

"What's wrong?"

"I couldn't do that," he said.

"Why not?"

"It wouldn't be right."

Roy was definitely a man of few words.

"Because . . ."

"I'd never betray Lisa."

"But Roy, Lisa could well have been the one who killed Edgar. Whatever your loyalties—"

"Get the hell out of here before I call the police."

She didn't have to be told twice.

Chapter 12

Leigh Ann was pouting. Teri was curiously quiet. April was hungry. And Monique was simply Monique. When Jennifer finally got to her critique meeting a full twenty minutes late Monday night, she dumped her umbrella (rain was threatening) and her briefcase on the floor.

Everyone was in her customary place, Leigh Ann on the sectional, April on the other sofa, Monique in her rocking chair, Teri stretching her long, brown legs on the floor. Jennifer could have sworn that girl had grown a full inch from all that yoga since she'd met her.

"Sorry. I've been running late all day," Jennifer apologized.

"We'd about decided you'd dropped out of the group," Leigh Ann declared. "You didn't even bother to call anyone when you didn't show up last Monday."

"It's been a rough couple of weeks. I fell asleep." Which was true. She'd sat down to try to get a few pages written before last week's meeting, and woke up at three in the morning cradling the keyboard.

"Have a brownie," April offered. "I brought them. They're cherry-cream cheese."

As Jennifer slumped down next to Teri, she reached toward the plate of brownies.

"Don't you reward her," Leigh Ann declared, leaning forward and swatting at Jennifer's fingers.

"What are you talking about?" Jennifer asked.

"Missing a meeting is one thing, but why didn't you tell us that you'd seen some dude get himself done in?" Teri was definitely mad, and she didn't anger easily; that is, unless Leigh Ann was involved.

"What are you talking about?" Jennifer asked innocently.

"Hah! As if you didn't know. 'Let's trade the industrial vat for a swimming pool. Make that chocolate syrup water.' I should have known you were pulling something on us."

"I thought it was clever," April observed, scooping brownie crumbs from the front of her shirt and eating them out of her hand.

The rocking stopped as Monique folded her hands and leaned forward. "Why don't you tell us about it, Jennifer? We understand that you witnessed Edgar Walker's murder."

Jennifer sighed. Well, she'd known all along they'd eventually find out about her presence at the Walker estate that night. But she hadn't expected them to be quite so touchy. Or to bungle the facts so badly. It looked as though she had no choice except to fess up. And apologize. She should have told them.

"I'm sorry. But I wasn't up to going into all the details that night, and I'm not a witness. That is, not to a murder. As a matter of fact, I didn't actually *witness* anything—"

"You know it would help if you could edit your speech as well as you do your writing," Teri observed, crossing her arms.

Jennifer sighed.

"She means she saw something, but she didn't see the murder," April explained, dusting her hands.

"So spill it," Leigh Ann insisted.

Briefly, Jennifer recounted her adventure at the Walker estate as succinctly as possible—without telling them the part about getting stuck in the fence.

"Wow. That crazy blonde pointed that shotgun straight at you?" Teri was definitely shaken, and, in view of this reminder of the mortal nature of life, apparently contrite as to how she'd treated Jennifer. She put a hand on her shoulder. "Weren't you scared?"

Jennifer could only nod, surprised by an unnatural catch in her throat.

Leigh Ann threw herself back against the sofa cushion and stared at the ceiling. "Just imagine being out there in the darkness, a bloodied body at your feet—"

"It was in the pool, and I couldn't see any blood—"

"The dew of late night moist against your skin. Your heart pounding so hard in your chest you can barely breathe. Fear tearing at your mind with the knowledge that somewhere out there in the shadows a cold-blooded killer was most likely watching, waiting . . ." She sat up. "You must have gone back to Macon, found Sam, and jumped his bones."

Jennifer closed her eyes and sighed. To Leigh Ann, *everything* was foreplay. "There's nothing sexy about finding a corpse or seeing the inside of a police station, let me assure you."

Leigh Ann snorted. "Nothing except all those gorgeous hunks in blue."

Jennifer should introduce Leigh Ann to Sweeney. Even *she* couldn't find anything sexy about that man! Or so she hoped.

"So, if Mrs. Walker didn't take out Edgar—he was that one in those disgusting commercials, right?" Teri asked.

"The very one," Jennifer assured her.

"So if she didn't kill him, how're you going to prove she didn't?"

As if all the burdens of the world had only one place to rest—directly on her shoulders.

"It's not Jennifer's place to do any such thing," Monique reminded them, always the voice of reason. "Mrs. Walker has hired attorneys to take care of that."

Ones who thought she should plead guilty.

"Of course it's not," April agreed, going for yet another brownie. "But if I know Jennifer, she will. Our girl feels guilty. She's got to assuage that guilt." She bit off half the chocolate square. "Man, these are good."

April turned her bright blue eyes on Jennifer. "So, what have you done?" she asked, as if addressing her two-year-old.

"I checked out the Down Home Grill," Jennifer offered. She wasn't about to tell the group what she'd found out about Roy.

"I ate there once," Leigh Ann confessed. "If they passed out blinders in the parking lot, it wouldn't be so bad. I mean, the food was quite good, but those bright, gawd-awful colors. You need to wear shades just to get in the door. Even the vinyl in the booths is a hot pink."

"That Eddie appetizer is scrumptious," April volunteered. "Wish I could get my hands on that steak sauce recipe."

April and most of the world.

"Tell us what you found out at the restaurant." Monique was definitely getting impatient.

"Not much. Some of their staff have quit because of the

murder. I did get a chance to look through some of the files, but then Lisa threw me out."

"Physically?" Leigh Ann leaned forward, as if hoping for news of a cat fight.

"No, not physically."

She slumped back into the cushions. "Oh."

"And Mrs. Walker's attorneys said I shouldn't go back," Jennifer added.

"And you shouldn't," April observed, now sucking on a bing cherry apparently left over from her brownie-making. She had a little bag of the fruit cradled against her stomach. "By the way, I tried your suggestions. I've got the first few pages of a story using that flying squirrel idea, and I'm writing it at about third grade level. I think I like it. I'll bring in some to read next week."

"You know, I could do that if I wanted to," Leigh Ann threw in.

"Do what? Write a story about a squirrel?" Teri asked.

"Get a job at that restaurant."

Jennifer cringed. The last thing she wanted was Leigh Ann snooping around and putting herself in danger. She had all the subtlety of a steamroller.

"No way! You wouldn't let her do that, would you?" Teri was not one to hide her feelings. "I'm surprised she's let out without supervision as it is. She should never go in there alone. We'd be fishing her body out of the Ocmulgee."

"No. It'd be far too dangerous for her alone," Jennifer agreed, "and I certainly can't go."

April made a sucking sound and another cherry disappeared. "Well, you can't expect me to go with her." She patted her belly.

Teri grabbed her feet and pulled them toward her torso,

bouncing her knees rapidly like butterfly wings, as all the eyes in the room turned toward her.

Teri's knees were suddenly still. "Whoa-ho! You think I'm going to haul myself all the way to Atlanta after putting in a full day's work to keep the likes of *her* out of trouble?" Teri stuck out her chin in Leigh Ann's direction. "You must be out of your cotton-pickin' minds." Her knees resumed their flutter, even faster this time.

"The decor is the pits," Leigh Ann said, "but the waitresses have cute little embroidered peasant blouses, with loose black pants and pink print sashes. How's about six, Wednesday afternoon?"

"Make it six-thirty. And I'm driving," Teri insisted.

"Fine. I'd just as soon not put the miles on my car."

"And you're paying for the gas."

"I'll pay for the gas," Jennifer offered. It was the least she could do.

It was a harrowing thought—Leigh Ann and Teri at the Down Home Grill, but once those two made up their minds, there would be no deterring them, regardless of the consequences. Not only was a murderer loose in Atlanta, but it was best to keep Leigh Ann and Teri away from sharp objects and breakables. The last time the two of them had done some undercover work for her, they'd almost set a building on fire.

Still, access to the restaurant was essential. She had to have someone on the inside. Much of Edgar's life and maybe his death centered around his business, and Lisa was not about to let her set foot through those doors.

"Promise me," Jennifer said, her throat constricting. "Promise me you'll be careful." She already felt some responsibility for Mrs. Walker's plight. If anything happened to Leigh Ann or Teri, she'd never forgive herself.

Chapter 13

Dear Contributor:

Thank you for sharing your work with Pen and Paper, Inc. We find ourselves acquiring very few new clients in the current competitive market. After reviewing your work, we're sorry to say we simply cannot take it on.

We wish you every success with another agency that can give it their wholehearted attention.

Good luck.

They—the faceless, nameless, antecedentless *they* on the other end of the postal chain—hadn't even bothered to date or sign the form letter. *They* could be the cleaning crew, for all Jennifer knew.

She sent the paper and its envelope skidding across her dining table. Then she examined the twenty pages of Maxie's second adventure, which she'd included with her brilliant query letter.

Hah! They hadn't even read it. The paper clip hadn't been moved (she could tell from the small dent it made in the paper), and the pages were as even as when they'd come from the printer. She riffled through the sheets to make absolutely sure. Clean.

She tossed the sheets after the letter and poured herself a steaming mug of black coffee. What a way to start a Friday, or any day, for that matter! She collapsed into a chair, tears welling in her eyes.

How dare they!

Rejections were always hard, but some were easier than others. The ones that left her manuscript with coffee stains, bent corners, pages upside down, cat prints, or peanut-butter smudges—those she could tolerate. At least some-one had looked at them, eaten over them, wiped up spills with them.

The kind she'd just gotten, slipped neatly back into her self-addressed, stamped envelope with only a form letter added, were intolerable. She might as well go to the post office and mail her query to herself. Cut out the middle man and save half the postage.

So they weren't accepting new clients. Well, she bet that if she were John Grisham, they'd make an exception.

She took a hot swig and almost choked. She hated black coffee, and she'd been drinking a whole lot of it in the past few weeks.

So now she was supposed to be creative, to go to her computer and write an inspired chapter. Heck, she hadn't even devised a plan to get that scumball victim of hers out of that vat of chocolate. Right now she'd like to add the entire staff of Pen and Paper to the mix. How long could they tread chocolate?

Well, her murder victim could stay there until he hard-ened into the biggest truffle of all time for all she cared. She was giving up writing. She would never again put pen to paper or finger to keyboard.

Never.

She would find something else to do with her life, something worthwhile, something noble, something that didn't require postage. She was far too creative to be wasting her talents and the precious hours of her days toiling away at stories that no one read and that no one appreciated. She would never write again.

At least not until much later that afternoon.

Muffy sauntered over, laid her head in Jennifer's lap, and whimpered. Doggy ESP. People should be so perceptive. She realized her fingers were cramping around the mug. Loosening her grip, she set the cup down and stroked the dog's muzzle.

She needed to get out, away from her apartment for a while. Relax. Maybe take a leisurely drive someplace. So what if she hadn't gotten her required number of pages written for today or yesterday or this week for that matter. She had no deadlines. Besides, she was giving up writing. She was free as a bird, and it was time to fly the coop.

She stood up just as the phone rang. It was Teri.

"I don't have but a second. My boss is in some big meeting, and they may call me in any minute, and I didn't call you last night because Leigh Ann and I didn't get home from the Grill until almost one." Teri gasped for breath. "Anyway, I snuck in and got a quick look at Lisa's file. Her maiden name was Mayfield, and she came to work at the Grill about ten and a half years ago."

"That would put her there maybe six months or so before Emma filed for divorce."

"Whatever. Anyway, I got her original address, a rural route in Lorraine."

"That's only a few miles south of Macon."

"Right."

"So what should I do?"

"Check it out, girl. Don't give me that. Go play P.I."
Then Teri gasped. "Gotta go." And the dial tone hummed
in her ear.

It was a beautiful day, and maybe a nice drive would be
relaxing.

Mrs. Walker had ordered her to stay out of the case, but
a little visit to Lisa's hometown of Lorraine could hardly
count. Besides, she drove down there all the time—at least
once every two years or so on her way to get peaches.

It was lovely country, and if she didn't blink, she
wouldn't miss the tiny bit of a town not much more than
spitting distance from Macon.

Jennifer parked her Bug in front of the Lorraine Post
Office, a small, brick building on the corner, and got out. A
bell rang over the door when she entered.

"Mornin'." A cheery, plump, middle-aged woman with
hair piled haphazardly onto her head greeted her from behind the counter. "Hot, don't ya think?" The words came
with a curious yet friendly stare over a small pair of
reading glasses.

Jennifer nodded.

"What can I do for you?" she asked, putting down the
stack of mail she had been sorting and leaning on the
counter with both arms.

Jennifer adopted a shy smile. Maxie had been an actress. How hard could it be?

"I'm working on my family tree," she drawled, pushing
the Southern lilt a bit past her normal speech. "I think
some of my distant relatives may have settled in this area.
You wouldn't happen to know . . ."

"I know most everyone who lives in this zip code and
pretty much all of their kin. Who you got in mind?" The

woman could as easily have been a bartender asking her what she'd have to drink.

"It's my great-grandmother's family, actually."

"Name?"

"Mayfield."

The woman's smile faded a little. "Oh."

Oh?

"If it's the Abraham Mayfield family you want, your best bet would be Melissa Bordeaux. She's what you might call the reigning matriarch of the clan and the sanest one of the lot. If anyone's likely to know who's related to who in that tangled group, it'd be her."

"And where would I find Ms. Bordeaux?"

For several seconds the woman stared at her as though sizing her up. "Tell you what. I'll give her a quick call and see if she's up to a visit this mornin'." A polite way of saying: *I have no intention of giving out her address without her permission.*

Jennifer tried nonchalantly to busy herself by looking about the place, all the while straining to overhear the phone conversation. But the woman turned her back and spoke so softly, she couldn't make out a word.

When the woman turned back to her, she was wearing a smile. "This morning's fine. Stay south on the main road about four miles, hang a left at the fork, and then take a right at the mailbox that looks like a miniature barn. And keep an eye out for Benjamin."

"Who's Benjamin?"

"The goat. He's penned in the yard. Go to the side door, not through the fence. 'Cause he'll butt if you turn your back on him."

Classy.

* * *

Sweet. Melissa Bordeaux seemed every bit as sweet as the banana cake she handed to Jennifer with a dollop of real whipped cream, even if she did keep the meanest billy goat Jennifer had ever come across. When she'd bent to admire the beautifully tended flowers, he'd almost gotten her through the fence that surrounded most of the old, weather-beaten farmhouse. Fortunately, the back porch had been left free for people to come and go.

The old lady leaned forward in her slipcovered chair and freshened Jennifer's coffee.

"I don't rightly see how your great-grandmother could be related to us, Miss . . ."

"Marsh," Jennifer supplied on reflex, catching herself just a tad too late. She should have cut out her tongue before this visit. She'd hoped to get by without having to give a name.

"Yes, well, Miss Marsh, my family doesn't seem to have misplaced any of our kinfolk. You say she was abducted by Indians at the age of seven?"

"Native Americans, actually." As if using the politically correct term would somehow make up for accusing a proud and honest people of kidnapping. Jennifer shifted on the old sofa. "Actually, she may have simply been lost. Yes, I think that was it."

The woman seemed to be considering this possibility.

"Or crazy," Jennifer added, confident that the insanity apparent in her great-grandmother's offspring would lend an air of authenticity to her story. She bit her lip. She'd been talking too much again, a major character flaw.

Maxie would never have let the conversation get so out of hand. She was there to *get* information, not give it. "You were telling me about your family," Jennifer reminded her, stuffing another bite of cake into her mouth to ensure she kept quiet.

"We've got family all over central and southern Georgia doing just about anything you can think of to do. Why, there's farmers, police, teachers, even got one down at the DMV. You name it, we've got it."

"Actually, I was more interested in the family right here in Lorraine, if it does turn out I'm related to you."

"I don't hardly know what to tell you. There was three of us girls and three boys that made it to adulthood. Me, of course. I'm the eldest. I had two girls and a boy. I've got seven grandchildren and over fifteen great-grandchildren." The woman beamed her pride in the direction of a wall full of photographs.

"My sister Priscilla never married. 'Course, you wouldn't be interested in her. She went off to Tennessee, became a librarian, died 'bout two years back. My other sister, Dorothy, married Mitchell Billings. They moved up to Macon and had a passel of young-uns—eight, I think. Let me see for sure. There was Petey, Pansy, Butch . . ."

This was like sorting BBs. But Melissa would have to get to the boys eventually.

"My brother Ralph was killed in the war. Buster married young and had three girls. And when Lester finally did get around to marrying, he and Lucille only had the one son."

So Lester's son *had* to be Lisa's father, unless this whole conversation had been for naught and Lisa was from some wayward branch of the Mayfield family tree.

"Wow!" Jennifer exclaimed. "You must have *some* family reunions."

"Every summer. Of course, the number gets smaller each year," she admitted sadly. "The young-uns—they

don't go in so much for family." She stretched over and
patted Jennifer's hand. "That's one reason I'm so glad to
help you out, a fine young woman like yourself, looking
for your roots."

Melissa shoved her glasses farther up her nose, inspected
Jennifer's face, and shook her head. "You're a mite pretty
little thing, but I just don't see any family resemblance."

The woman pushed up from her armchair and got her
cane under her hand. She was taller than Jennifer had realized, and more muscular than fleshy. Still, she strained to
take her first step, and Jennifer put down her cake to help.

"No, you sit still," Melissa ordered. "I'll be fine once I
get going. This arthritis is not going to be what stops me."

She managed the few steps to the paneled wall that was
covered with family photos in cheap frames and plucked
down a large, color shot. She balanced on the cane as she
ran her hands over the glass, sending dust floating to the
floor. Then she brought it back and offered it to Jennifer.

"This was the last really big reunion. Must have been
fifteen, sixteen years ago. One of Dorothy's sons was
working at a photography studio that year. He had one
made for each of the brothers and sisters. Take a look at it.
I don't think you'll see anybody that looks anything like
you."

Jennifer scanned the photo. The older folks had been
caught laughing, smiling. There was Melissa, younger,
straighter, darker hair, her arms circling an older man who
held himself steady with a cane. She skimmed the teenagers
on their knees in the second row and their younger siblings
directly in front of them, her eyes drawn immediately to
the far left—that had to be Lisa. But her hair was dark and
her face looked fresh and soft and sweet.

"And the food that year! My goodness!" Melissa let out

a guffaw as she collapsed back into her chair. "You've never seen or tasted anything like it! Even the young folk brought in their best dishes. Many of them were in 4-H, and most nearly all of them participated in the county fair, girls and boys alike. Blue ribbons, reds, whites—we took them all."

The banana cake was definitely worthy of a best of show, as Jennifer knew after making desserts and pastries for Dee Dee's catering business.

"This cake is utterly delicious," Jennifer agreed.

"Won two years in a row, 1957 and 1958. I retired it after that. Time to give someone else a chance."

"I'd love to have the recipe."

The smile dropped from Melissa's face. Immediately, Jennifer realized she had crossed into sacred ground.

"I don't give out my recipes."

"I'm sorry. I didn't realize . . ."

The smile returned. "Of course you didn't. That's all right."

Melissa eased herself next to Jennifer on the couch. "But you see what I mean?" She laughed. "I don't see anyone that looks the least bit like you in that picture. No taffy-colored hair."

There was a familiarity within the group, some shared roundness of features, a bend to the nose, something that gave them that family look.

"Who's this?" Jennifer asked, casually pointing out Lisa.

"Now she was some young-un. Lester's granddaughter. Found the cosmetics store before she was tall enough to reach the counter. She was Lorraine's Miss Peach her senior year in high school. Pretty little thing, but with a tendency to gain weight. You could tell even then. Sweet child."

Yeah, *real* sweet.

"What happened to her?"

"We're right proud of her. She and her husband run that chain of Edgar's Down Home Grills. I always knew that girl would be something special, that one. Yes siree. Something special."

Jennifer had to agree that Lisa was, indeed, *special.* Anyone who could instill that much fear could not be described as average.

She put her plate on the coffee table and stood up. What had she expected to find in Lorraine anyway? Early evidence of Lisa's homicidal tendencies? "I've got to go," she said.

"So soon? We were just getting acquainted."

Jennifer nodded her head. "I had to flip the lever for the reserve tank in my Volkswagen, so I need to get to a gas station before I run out of gas." She'd used that excuse before. The logic didn't hold, but the trick was to get out before the person she was talking to had enough time to think about what she was saying.

Melissa walked her out and stood on the porch as Jennifer opened the car door. "Now isn't that the cutest little thing. I haven't seen one of those Bugs in a coon's age."

"Thanks again," Jennifer called as she turned the car around.

She pulled out of the dirt driveway and took off for Macon feeling strangely unsettled. She couldn't shake the feeling that in her encounter with Melissa Bordeaux, somehow she'd given more than she'd gotten.

Chapter 14

Maxie watched as the crane swung over the huge industrial vat and lowered the leather harness toward the milky chocolate. One uniformed policeman strained from his position atop a step ladder and prodded the bobbing mass in the direction of another officer who, with his sleeves rolled and elbows chocolate deep, cursed as he draped the harness about the body. Licking his fingers, he gave the okay, and the machinery groaned as the body was pulled from the brown goo, dripping like an oversized bonbon.

Rinnnnnng. Rinnnnnng. Rinnnnnng.

Maxie turned, her nose thumping into the chest of police sergeant Oscar Mobley. "You still here?" he asked, not bothering to hide his irritation.

"I'm working security. You know that," she chided.

"You were working security. Your employer is now a giant Milky Way bar."

It was true. Rufus Donaldson was dead, but he'd given her a retainer like she'd never seen before, and she owed him at least a month's work, a month she intended to see that he got.

Rinnnnnng. Rinnnnnng. Rinnnnnng.

"What's that infernal ringing?" Mobley asked.

"Must be a glitch in the machinery," Maxie offered.

Rinnnnnng. Rinnnnnng. Rinnnnnng.

Muffy woofed lazily at Jennifer's feet, stretched, and, whining, sauntered over to the door. Jennifer pushed back from the computer and raked away the mess of hair that was tangled over her forehead.

Oh, crud. The doorbell.

She glanced at her watch. Five minutes after seven. It couldn't be! After she'd gotten back from Lorraine, she'd grabbed a sandwich and sat down to write for just a few minutes. She must have dropped into some kind of time warp. Was it tonight that she'd invited Sam over for dinner?

She ran to the door and peered through the peephole. It was him all right, and he'd even brought wine and a gardenia.

She unlocked the door and opened it a crack, letting her hair dangle in her face. "Stay right where you are," she ordered, slammed it back, almost catching Muffy's nose, and fled to the bathroom. The dog, now convinced something was up, was hot on her heels.

She wiped the bands of smudged mascara from under her eyes, applied a fresh coat, quickly lined her mouth with lipstick, and dragged a brush through her uncooperative hair, flipping it away from her face.

Cripes. She had no idea what she was going to serve him for dinner.

She raced back to the door and checked. He was still there, patiently examining the petals of the flower.

Shyly, she again cracked the door and peeked through the slit.

"Writing?" he asked with a smirk.

Hah! He thought he knew her so well.

She opened the door wider and pulled him inside.

"What makes you think that?"

He looked her up and down, and Jennifer followed his gaze over her clothes. Sleeveless flannel shirt, blue jeans, socks, no shoes.

"I don't see any paint buckets or brushes. So what's Maxie been up to today?" he asked, handing her the flower, brushing past her and setting the wine down on the coffee table.

She breathed in the sweetness of its scent. Then she quickly found a bowl, filled it with water, and floated the white flower. She put it in the middle of the coffee table, where the heady scent could perfume the air.

"Maxie was rejected again today," she said as casually as she could manage, her chin quivering involuntarily.

Without a word, Sam folded her to him. For a long moment they stood there. When she tried to pull away, he drew her back.

"I'm sorry," he whispered.

As if somebody had died.

She shook him off. She didn't need anybody understanding her quite that well. "I'm fine," she lied. "Really I am."

"So, you *were* writing."

"A little."

"Good."

Why was his saying that so irritating? As if all she had to do was *do* it. Simply string words together.

She collapsed on the sofa, hugging a pillow to her. Better to have some distance between them, either because she was feeling particularly vulnerable at the moment or because she was likely to bite his head off if he said . . .well, almost anything.

He loosened his tie. "So what's for dinner?"

Like that.

"Well . . ." she began, staring at him from under her eyelashes. "I've got macaroni and cheese in a box. Estimated preparation time: fifteen minutes. Or, I could make an omelet: twenty minutes. Or vegetarian fried rice: closer to thirty. I'll have to make the rice. Or—"

"You forgot I was coming over."

"Completely. I'm so sorry." And she meant it. Her actions—actually, her lack of actions—were inexcusable.

He looked pensive, as though considering the implications of her candor. "I could take this personally, you know."

She nodded. "Don't. I treat all my friends horribly." Look what she'd done to Mrs. Walker. "I don't mean to, really."

He joined her on the couch, slouching into the cushions and propping his feet next to the wine bottle. He fished in his jacket pocket and came up with a mangled package of miniature powdered sugar doughnuts, which he tossed onto the table. "Those will keep us from starving. At least for a little while."

"I'll make it up to you," she promised. "I'll have the Thai House deliver some of those wonderful peanut noodles we're so fond of. I'll give them a call, after you've had a minute to relax."

He let his eyes drift shut. He was obviously tired. Searching out the truth and reporting it to the readership of the *Macon Telegraph* was a demanding job.

"I was surprised to see you at Emma's," she commented. She never had found out what he was doing there.

"Yeah, well, she asked me to come."

"Because . . ."

"Because she knew I was gathering information for an

article on franchise fraud. I'd done some research at the Grill because of Edgar's plans to take his restaurants national."

"National?" Jennifer sat up.

Sam's eyes popped open. "I thought you knew."

She shook her head. "Why would he do that? He already had the two here in Macon, three in Atlanta, and one in Marietta. How many more could he handle?"

"None. He was going to franchise. You know, sell the concept—the decor, Edgar's Special Steak Sauce, the Eddie. I suspect all the local sites would be sold, too, except, perhaps, the original restaurant."

"And he'd become the supplier."

"For each and every restaurant."

Jennifer took a deep breath. "That could easily be worth millions."

"Easily. If it flew."

Jennifer suddenly had a vision of turquoise and pink stucco dotting America, and herds upon herds of cattle headed for extinction. She shuddered.

"I guess Edgar's choice of cuisine is a little hard for you to take," he said, as if reading her mind.

"Vegetarianism is a personal choice. I don't expect to impose it on the whole world."

He shrugged out of his coat, twisted, and tossed it over the back of the sofa toward a dining room chair. It missed its mark, and Muffy immediately lay down on it.

Jennifer leaped up, shooed the dog away, and hung the coat on the back of the chair.

She settled back down next to Sam and snuggled under his arm. Then she reached over for the phone, punched in the numbers with her thumb, and placed an order for the noodles and Sam's favorite, garlic chicken, adding a pint of coconut ice cream.

"So what did you turn up at the restaurant?" he asked as she settled back and he stroked her hair.

Silver-tongued devil. No wonder she couldn't resist him.

At least *she* knew how to be romantic—thanks to Leigh Ann's torrid prose. She started at his chin and outlined his jaw with little kisses between each word. "My replacement—Roy—is making really big bucks." When she got to his ear, he squirmed.

"How big?"

She considered seeing how ticklish he really was but decided instead to rest her head in the crook of his neck.

"Megabucks. A hundred grand."

She could feel his body tense. He must be stunned. But then big money was always hard for a writer to comprehend.

"And he wasn't the only one." She nuzzled his neck and felt him relax. "Edgar had hired a special consultant who was making fifty."

"Natalie Brewster. She just might be worth it."

Now that was a mood-breaking comment if she'd ever heard one. Jennifer sat up. "You know her?"

"Sure. She was my liaison concerning the franchise. Very friendly, beautiful woman. About your height, long dark hair, emerald eyes, ivory complexion, terrific figure."

Nice of him to notice. Lisa must have really been fond of her. Jennifer had never met her, and she hated the woman already.

"I don't suppose you could tell from your conversations with her"—assuming there had been dialogue—"whether she was any good at her job."

"She was great. MBA from Emory."

The fifty grand was beginning to look a lot more reasonable. She'd noticed a college transcript in her file but hadn't had time to look at it.

"She told me Edgar hired her specifically to develop the concept for the franchise. She plans to alter the color scheme."

Thank goodness for that. Maybe the woman had some taste.

"And play up the family angle," Sam added.

"I didn't see her at the restaurant."

"Could be she doesn't work out of there. I interviewed her at her apartment."

Unprofessional. Not to mention cozy.

"So you think she truly is a consultant, even though she's salaried?"

"Well, yeah. I can't imagine her working in the middle of the mayhem of some restaurant, especially that one."

One that came with a Lisa.

"Seems strange no one's mentioned her."

"True, but why would they? I'll give her a call."

Jennifer handed him the phone. No reason for him to go all the way home when he could as easily call from her apartment.

Sam went to his jacket pocket and took a business card from a card holder. He punched in the numbers, waited several seconds, and then hung up.

"No answer," Jennifer observed.

"And no machine."

"And you don't like it," she added.

He shook his head.

"She's probably just out."

This time he nodded.

"But you're still concerned."

Again he nodded.

"Okay. First thing tomorrow morning, you and me in Atlanta, knocking on her door."

"You sure you want to go with me? Don't you have writing to do?"

"Don't you have newspaper work to do?"

"Tomorrow is Saturday. Besides, this *is* newspaper work."

"I'll be ready by seven."

Sam might need her help. This was, after all, a murder investigation. She wasn't about to let him go in there alone. Who knew what Sam might run into at Natalie Brewster's apartment?

Chapter 15

Natalie Brewster was doing quite well for someone only a few years out of grad school. Her apartment, in a gated luxury community only a few blocks from the Grill, made Jennifer's modest digs in Macon look downright squalid, at least from the outside. Not that she'd compare herself to a woman whose name Sam couldn't mention without breathing hard.

Sam leaned on the doorbell one more time, the bright morning sunshine glinting off the brass trim. He was looking a bit distressed, a cute furrow ruffling his brow, his eyes a lighter blue than normal.

"Do you think something's wrong?" Jennifer asked.

"Not necessarily." He seemed to be reassuring himself as much as her. "I just don't like it when one person dies and then I have trouble finding another."

Okay. She could buy that one. "Maybe we should check with the guard. He should have seen her leave if she went out this morning."

"Yeah. But in that case, he should have stopped us on the way in." They had scooted right past him. Sam and his car were on the visitors list.

Sam tried the knob but it was locked. He nodded and they headed back to the security station.

"Miz Brewster," the guard repeated, taking off his cap and running his hand over his bald head. "No, sir, I haven't seen her."

And he would have remembered, too. Jennifer could tell. Interesting effect this woman had on men. "How about yesterday?" She leaned across Sam so she could see the guard better through the driver's window.

The man shook his head. "I don't recollect seeing her for some time, now that you mention it. I come on at seven and go off at three. Could be I've just been missing her. 'Course she could be out on one of those business trips she takes now and again, but she usually tells me when she's going off."

"Would you know where to?" Sam asked.

The man rubbed his chin. He seemed to be sizing the two of them up. "Remember I didn't say for sure she was gone. What kind of business you got with her?"

They weren't going to get any more out of this guy, especially if he found out he was talking to a reporter. Jennifer flashed him a smile. "Thanks for your help."

She waved as Sam pulled away and headed down the street.

"Tell me about this woman," she ordered.

"I did. She's gor—"

"Not her physical attributes." She'd already had enough of that. Besides, if she'd asked about one of his male friends, would he lead off with how the man looked? She thought not.

"Bright, personable, confident, competent."

Okay, the woman was perfect. They could worship at her shrine later, but she wasn't going to buy the competent part so easily. Competency could be faked. What did Sam know about the franchise business? "So how'd Edgar find her?"

"I don't know. It didn't come up."

"Okay. Then who was involved with the franchise plans?"

"Natalie has been working on it over the last six months, handling most of it herself—developing a training program, calculating the investment necessary, finding the franchisees—"

"Is that a word? Franchisee?"

"Yeah. Look it up. From what he said, Edgar had pretty much put the development of the plan in her hands."

Her competent and lovely hands.

"They were looking for area developers."

"Come again?"

"People who want more than one restaurant. They put up the money, hire managers, and coordinate matters so their own restaurants are never in competition with one another."

Jennifer whistled. "Big bucks."

"Excuse me?"

"Big bucks—that's what it takes to open several restaurants at one time."

"You ain't kidding."

"And a lot of expertise."

"Nope. As a matter of fact, they look for people who don't have any restaurant experience. That way—"

"They can train them the way they want the operation to run."

"Right."

"Which requires something else."

He cocked his head.

"A lot of trust."

Sam nodded. "Not to mention work. Natalie kept insisting she didn't have time to talk with me even though Edgar had personally arranged the interview after Emma called him. I got her to outline the process, but that was about it. She gave me the brush-off."

Sam could be a bit overbearing at times, especially when he was pushing for information. But usually he didn't brush off easily.

"They're gonna want their money," she said.

"Who?"

"The franchisees."

Sam shook his head as he stopped at the light. "I'm not even sure money has passed hands yet. But even if it has, the business is continuing to thrive. Why wouldn't it go forward?"

Jennifer shrugged. "Who knows what Edgar's will specifies."

"I'll continue to try to locate Natalie and also see what I can find out about the investors."

"And check into her background," Jennifer suggested.

"Why?"

"Sounds like Edgar entrusted his entire future to this woman. I'd like to know more about her." She wasn't about to add that she didn't trust her simply on principle. After all, she had green eyes just like Leigh Ann.

"Okay. And what's your plan?"

"I've got an inside source I plan to cultivate. Someone who should be able to tell me a lot about what's been going on at the Down Home Grill."

Chapter 16

"Nice of you to take me out for breakfast like this, Ms. Marsh," Suzy commented, "and to my favorite restaurant, too, not counting the Grill, of course. I even thought about calling you, you having connections with Mrs. Emma Walker and her being the actual owner and all. Lisa doesn't much care for me . . ."

Suzy was cute, bubbly, friendly, pleasantly thin, not to mention really young. Obviously Lisa had issues.

" . . . and I'd really like to keep my job. Roy and me . . ." She blushed charmingly. "I know he's a little old for me, but . . ." She sighed and stared into space as if looking at twinkling stars.

Jennifer couldn't help but follow her gaze. The Waffle House didn't hold much for the romantic, only an oozing of batter from a couple of overfilled waffle presses, two very harried waitresses, and a cook juggling eggs, bacon, sausage, and toast.

"He's really good-looking. Don't you think?" Suzy asked.

Jennifer cleared her throat and allowed a noncommittal tilt of her head. It was hard to get excited over someone who'd almost crowned her with a skillet.

"And he's *so* talented. I've worked in other restaurants,

and let me tell you, he's no slouch. The only thing he needs to make him perfect is one of those cute little sports cars." Suzy took a sip of her milk.

"I figure we'll have three children. One boy and two girls. He'll be a great daddy, and he's got good genes, too. He doesn't have any of those awful hereditary diseases in his family like diabetes or tuberculosis."

This was probably not the time to point out to Suzy that tuberculosis was not a hereditary disease.

"I've got arthritis on both sides," she rattled on. "A poor kid wouldn't have a chance if he got another dose from his father, you know what I mean. If you're gonna get serious about someone, you've got to know these things."

While Jennifer could understand Suzy's concerns for genetic perfection, she wasn't paying for breakfast to hear about Roy's chromosomes.

"So how did Lisa and Edgar get along?" Jennifer asked, as if that was what they'd been talking about all along.

"Not well. At least not anymore. They got into some rows. Word was there was someone else."

"Lisa was going out on Edgar?"

The girl vigorously shook her head. "Heck no. *Mister* Walker. He wanted a divorce, at least that's what Louise told me. She said she overheard them fighting like two mad dogs back in the office one afternoon."

So Edgar was moving on to number three. Well, the blush was definitely off of Lisa's peach. And once she'd turned testy, it was hard to say what she had in her favor.

"Who?" she asked, wondering if the dark hair and green eyes of Natalie Brewster had something to do with Edgar's change of heart. Edgar's craggy face had to get better looking with each potential franchise.

"Oh, Ms. Marsh. I don't like to gossip."

A waitress leaned across the booth and set down two plates, each dwarfed by an enormous pecan waffle. "Anything else?" she asked, refilling Jennifer's coffee cup.

"We're fine, thank you," Jennifer said.

"What about the waitresses?" she asked casually as their own waitress moved away. "Did Edgar show an interest in any of them?"

Suzy added so much syrup, the waffle swam in the sticky goo. "Are you kidding? Even if he had made a pass at one of them, nothing would have happened. They're all scared to death of Lisa."

She could understand that. "How about Natalie Brewster?"

"Oh, you mean that woman Mr. Walker brought in to talk about the franchise." Suzy speared a piece of waffle and let the syrup ooze off onto her paper place mat as she talked. "Could've been, I guess, though why a woman like that would be interested in a man like him . . ."

She'd already heard about Natalie's attributes from Sam. She didn't need Suzy confirming her goddess status.

"I don't mean any disrespect, Ms. Marsh. Mr. Walker was my employer."

"And how did Lisa feel about Natalie?" Jennifer asked.

"She kept her distance. Natalie would show up in her designer suits, looking like she'd stepped off the cover of *Glamour* magazine. So maybe there was somethin' there." Suzy shrugged. "Never no accountin' for taste."

True words.

"So how are things going at the restaurant? Are you still shorthanded?" If she couldn't get a more thorough report from Teri and Leigh Ann, maybe Suzy could tell her what they were up to.

Suzy took another bite of waffle and said, "Lisa hired three new girls."

At last. Except for that one hurried phone call from Teri, the two of them had been infuriatingly taciturn about what was going on at the restaurant. Neither had the decency to pick up a phone and fill her in. When Jennifer finally had gotten hold of Leigh Ann, she'd practically dozed off in the middle of the conversation, waking up with a halfhearted promise to call when she learned something. Working two jobs must be cutting into her nap time. And she wouldn't even see them tonight. Monique had unexpected company, so the meeting had been canceled.

"Having more staff should help," she said.

Suzy nodded. "One of them's real good. She's obviously waitressed before. But I don't know about the other two. There's something peculiar about them."

Jennifer almost choked on her food.

"You all right?" Suzy asked.

She swallowed what was in her mouth. "The other two girls—what's wrong with them?"

"Well, I don't rightly know, but I do know I don't like the little one, Leigh Ellen, Leigh something."

Jennifer had to bite her tongue to keep from saying Leigh Ann.

Suzy frowned. "I think she's taken a liking to Roy. I caught her with him backed up next to the freezer standing on her tippy toes and leaning into his chest."

Jennifer dropped her head. That girl needed more than a keeper. She needed a warden.

Suzy opened her big eyes wide. " 'Course, Roy insisted it was nothin', but I'm not sure I believe him."

Roy was not the one to worry about here.

"I've caught her talkin' to him—alone—a few other

times, batting those green eyes up at him." Suzy sighed. "He's just a man. It's not like he can take a lot of that."

Suzy had been reading too many romance novels, the kind that Leigh Ann wrote.

"You know what really made me suspicious?"

Jennifer could hardly wait to hear.

"Roy took Leigh off the main floor, put her in the kitchen as Gus's assistant."

"Cooking?"

Suzy nodded.

"With fire?"

Again she nodded.

"And knives?"

"What's wrong, Ms. Marsh? You're looking kind of gray."

"And what about the other one?"

"You mean the African American?"

"I guess so."

"She gives me the creeps. It's like she's always sneaking around, writing on her order forms even when she's not with a customer. And on napkins. Stuffing them into her pockets. I'm really beginning to wonder about her."

And with good reason. Jennifer had been wondering about Teri for a long time. "So what do you think she's up to?" she asked, casually taking a sip of coffee.

"I think she may be a spy."

Jennifer forced the liquid down her throat. "Really. How so?"

"Industrial espionage."

"Of what?"

"The sauce, of course. People would kill for that recipe."

The situation at the Grill was definitely getting out of

hand. Jennifer had no choice. She'd have to find a way to go back to the restaurant and see what was going on, but she couldn't do it right away. She had a dragon lady breathing down her neck.

Assistant District Attorney Arlene Jacobs had caught her just as she was leaving the house that morning to come to breakfast with Suzy. She wanted Jennifer in her office no later than tomorrow afternoon, and if she couldn't manage it on her own, Jacobs assured her, she'd be glad to send a police escort to see that she got there.

But before she saw Jacobs, Jennifer wanted some answers from the only person who could give them. She had to know what Mrs. Walker had been doing married to a classless crumb like Edgar Walker.

Chapter 17

"Edgar was quite handsome back then," Mrs. Walker confided. "More tea?" She gripped the handle of the elegant sterling silver teapot glinting from the late morning sunshine pouring in through the glass wall of her living room.

Jennifer had had enough tea to float the Spanish Armada, and she didn't even particularly like hot tea. Just the same, she smiled sweetly and nodded.

Whatever it took, she had to have at least some knowledge of the Walkers' relationship before she walked into that courthouse for her interview with Arlene Jacobs tomorrow afternoon.

Tiger growled furiously at her feet, whipping his head rapidly back and forth, his teeth clamped tightly about Jennifer's date book. She'd made the mistake of leaving her purse on the floor, and the beast was systematically dragging out each and every item, shaking it hard and spitting it out. But she would gladly sacrifice it all if only Mrs. Walker would tell her what she'd come there to hear.

"How is that handsome young man of yours?" Mrs. Walker asked, filling Jennifer's cup and changing the subject for the umpteenth time.

"Sam's not mine, but he's fine. You were—"

"I was so glad he could make it over here the other night. I've become quite fond of him." She pulled Jennifer's left hand away from her chin and stroked her ring finger. "Your hand would look so much lovelier with a bit of jewelry. Something simple. Perhaps a solitaire."

And this coming from a woman who was dumped after forty-five years of marriage! Mrs. Walker needed a reality check.

Jennifer snatched her hand away and shoved it under her. She did like things simple, one major lifestyle change at a time. The next one she was looking for was becoming a published novelist, not a bride, and definitely not a mother. *Just be quiet, Jaimie!*

And if Mrs. Walker liked Sam so much, *she* could marry him.

"Why the heck did you marry him?" Jennifer blurted out, unable to play the game one minute longer.

Mrs. Walker seemed startled. "Edgar, you mean?"

As if she were Elizabeth Taylor and had an assortment of ex-husbands to choose from.

Jennifer nodded. What she really wanted to do was bang her head against the table.

Tiger had abandoned the date book in favor of a tiny package of tissues, which he was shredding one by one.

"Oh." Mrs. Walker added more sugar to her cup and stirred briskly. "I suppose I loved him, although that was so long ago I hardly remember. I certainly thought I did. Why, he could charm the bark off a tree back then. And he was one good kisser, I can tell you that."

Ugh! What a thought. The image of Edgar standing next to that bull and grinning from ear to ear flooded her mind. She gave a little involuntary shudder, hoping Mrs. Walker wouldn't notice.

"I see you don't understand. Those awful television commercials. That was his publicist's idea." She clucked her tongue. "Tacky, tacky, tacky."

To match the restaurant's decor.

"Daddy didn't like him. Forbade me to marry him. But, unfortunately for me, he relented and gave us his blessing. I was barely nineteen, a child really. Have a cookie, dear."

Mrs. Walker shoved a small dessert plate filled with chocolate dipped shortbread in her direction. Reluctantly, she took one. She suspected Mrs. Walker wanted to fill her mouth to keep her from asking any more questions.

"You must have been proud of how well he did with the business," Jennifer prodded. Now that Mrs. Walker was finally talking about Edgar, she wasn't about to let her stop, cookie or no.

Mrs. Walker shook her head. "He didn't do at all well while we were married. The restaurant simply limped along. He'd get in trouble; I'd pour money into it. Things didn't start humming until after our split. After the Eddie and the special steak sauce. That's what made the whole business. The other restaurants all opened within the last six years."

Jennifer remembered when the first one came to Macon on Riverside Drive three years ago. A second had opened in the Shurlington area within six months or a year, but she had no idea that the other locations were so new.

"And already he was planning a national franchise?" she asked, popping the cookie whole into her mouth.

"Edgar wasn't getting any younger, dear. It was now or never for him, don't you see? He doesn't—didn't—" She stopped for a moment and composed herself. "He didn't need the money. He was in it for the sport, for the fun of it. It was a brilliant move."

The excitement in Mrs. Walker's voice was contagious. She was vibrant, alive. Why, if Jennifer didn't know better, she would think Mrs. Walker had been personally involved with the plan to franchise. What a silly idea.

"Will you go forward with the franchise?"

"Of course. But I'm afraid I'll have to wait until all this mess with Edgar's murder is settled."

"Have you spoken with Natalie Brewster?"

"You mean that lovely young woman Edgar hired?"

Jennifer nodded. Natalie seemed to come with her own list of adoring adjectives.

"No, I haven't. I hadn't even thought about it—although I suppose someone should. I'm sure she's anxious to know what will be expected of her now that Edgar's gone."

"There must be a lot of money involved."

"I should think so, and if Edgar actually received funds from people waiting to open their own Down Home Grills, their concerns will have to be addressed. Walter is handling all that."

"The profits should be considerable if everything goes all right. I don't suppose you know what'll happen to them."

"A good part of it will come to me. When Daddy gave Edgar the money to start the restaurant, he had the contracts drawn up so I owned the controlling share, fifty-one percent. Not that there were any returns to begin with, as I told you before."

There certainly were profits now. "Since Edgar's gone, who controls the other forty-nine? Won't it come to you through a partners' agreement?"

Mrs. Walker blinked hard. "Of course not, dear. My having the controlling share was enough for Edgar to swallow, particularly when I wasn't actually working in the restaurant. When we divorced, I had the partners' agreement voided. It only seemed fair. I'm quite sure he left everything to Lisa. But you could ask Walter Ornsby. He took care of the reading of the will. He might be able to tell you about Natalie Brewster as well. I believe he was the one who introduced her to Edgar."

"And what about you?"

"Me?"

"Who's your heir?" It was an intrusion, and the distaste in Mrs. Walker's face reflected Jennifer's lack of tact. But she didn't have another two hours to wrangle it out of her. Women were funny. They would volunteer the most intimate details of their sex lives, but don't ask how much money they or their husbands made or how much they paid for their houses. And, in this case, who they left their money to. As if everybody wouldn't know the minute they died.

"Actually, my sister's twins, Babs and Benny. You met them here the other night. It's even possible Edgar may have left them something as well since they each manage one of the restaurants. Ask Walter when you talk to him. They're all the family either one of us has. Before he married Lisa, they were his heirs, too."

Ah, yes. That second pesky marriage to Lisa. She'd been pushing her luck as it was, but Jennifer had to know about the breakup. She had to know why the Walkers divorced and Edgar had married Lisa—besides the obvious. The question was how she could ask without upsetting the ex-Mrs. Walker.

Jennifer absently selected another cookie, pulling off some of the chocolate coating and savoring it on her tongue. "How do you feel about Lisa?" she said offhandedly, as if asking Emma to pass the cream.

Mrs. Walker pointed her spoon at Jennifer, and for a moment she was afraid the woman might bop her on the nose with it. Instead it clattered to the table.

"I'm sorry, dear," Mrs. Walker apologized. "How clumsy of me."

Neither spoke for several seconds.

"I suppose I owe you some explanation," Mrs. Walker began, "as caught up in this mess as you are."

She didn't, but Jennifer wasn't about to tell her that, especially after she'd earned an explanation by drinking close to a gallon of tea and letting Tiger salivate all over her new tube of Honey Rose lipstick. Like she was ever going to use that again.

"Lisa started at the restaurant as a waitress—goodness, it must have been eleven or so years ago now. Edgar and I were having some problems. The business was in another rough period, and I found myself once more dipping into savings to bail it out. The man had had more than enough years to get his act together, and I was ready to sell and be done with that expensive hobby of his. As you can imagine, our personal relationship was suffering under the strain."

Jennifer nodded sympathetically. Most marriages did, at one time or another, have some problems—and those didn't have Edgar and his bull as part of the partnership.

"Edgar sought the . . . comfort he couldn't find at home someplace else."

"With Lisa," Jennifer offered.

"With Lisa. I thought she was shamefully young, barely twenty. I didn't blame her even though I haven't always been kind in my comments about her."

"So they had an affair."

Mrs. Walker nodded.

"And I suppose he asked for a divorce."

"Oh, no, dear. Edgar begged for forgiveness. I insisted on the divorce. I could and did put up with a lot from that man over the years, but I would not tolerate infidelity. Not again."

Mrs. Walker did not strike Jennifer as the sort of woman a man would run around on. But then, Edgar didn't strike Jennifer as the sort of man Mrs. Walker would marry.

"Edgar had strayed before?" She almost whispered the words.

Emma looked her straight in the eye. "There's an old saying, 'Fool me once, shame on you. Fool me twice, shame on me.' It happened."

She paused for a moment as if searching her memory. "I guess it had to be thirty years or so ago now. I was terribly hurt, but Daddy was still alive then."

Why was it so hard to admit when a parent was right? Jennifer shook her head. To suffer through a life with an Edgar Walker because her parents had disapproved—

"I took Edgar back," Mrs. Walker went on. "When it happened with Lisa, both of my parents were dead, of course, and I wasn't about to put up with such nonsense. I threw him out. Within months they were married. I let them run the business. I really had very little interest in it outside of collecting a check now and then. About three years later, the Eddie was born and the profits began to pick up. Their success became my success.

"They created a whole new look and image for the place. The mauve and navy blue decor I had selected was scrapped for the turquoise and hot pink. They stuccoed the walls. I thought it looked like it should serve Mexican food or at least Tex-Mex, but it remained a steak house. They even put in a long saltwater tank, which I thought was pretty silly since they don't even serve seafood. Edgar liked fish—to watch, not to eat—and I never let him have a tank in the house. I guess Lisa wouldn't, either."

"Tell me about the Eddie," Jennifer prompted.

"I hardly know what to tell. It's every man's idea of heaven on a plate, incredibly fatty and utterly delicious."

"And the steak sauce? When did that come about?"

"At the same time. It was so popular with the appetizer that Edgar decided to serve it separately."

"And you still don't know what's in it?'

Mrs. Walker shook her head. "I thought Edgar was the only one who knew, but obviously I was wrong. The restaurant is still open, still serving the sauce. Lisa must have the recipe, because without it, Edgar's Down Home Grill would long ago have had to close its doors."

So Mrs. Walker didn't know that Roy made the sauce.

"Tell me." Jennifer leaned in close. "What were you doing at Edgar's that night?"

Mrs. Walker's bright eyes suddenly grew wide. "Doing?" she asked innocently.

"Doing."

"You really must have another cookie," she insisted, shoving the plate in Jennifer's direction.

Obviously, the woman was embarrassed, and why shouldn't she be? "Mae Belle already told me about the chickens and the dye you put in the pool."

"Chickens?"

Jennifer nodded. "I know you were playing pranks."

Mrs. Walker let out a sigh and once again seemed quite friendly. "Oh, of course, the pranks. Yes, I was playing pranks." She laughed like a silly little girl.

"What kind?"

"What kind of what?"

"Pranks." She might as easily have been asking "Who's on first?"

"Well, let's see. I'm not sure quite what it was I had decided upon this time when someone struck me from behind. And then I forgot all about it, of course, with the police standing right there."

And Edgar dead. But she had no props with her that night. No spray paint, no living creatures, no dyes, at least none that Jennifer had seen and none that the police called to anyone's attention. And the strange way Mrs. Walker was acting suggested that she might have been at the estate for another reason that night, a reason she had no intention of sharing with Jennifer or anybody else.

Chapter 18

If Arlene Jacobs didn't stop pressing that pencil that was woven through her fingers, it was liable to splinter into pieces and hit her in the eye. And if she stuck her tongue any deeper into her cheek, it could well peek right on through her skin.

"Come again," Jacobs demanded, as if she couldn't quite believe what she was hearing.

Well, if the woman didn't want to hear what she had to say, she should never have called her to her office.

"Just because I saw the knife, doesn't mean Emma Walker used it."

"You saw it and she used it." Jacobs leaned forward in her chair across her large, wooden desk.

Very aggressive posturing, Jennifer thought, but it would take more than a five-foot-two-inch assistant D.A. to intimidate her. "It's been proven over and over again what poor testimony eyewitnesses give. Erle Stanley Gardner pointed out time and again—"

"You were *there*. You knew Emma Walker personally. She did not attempt to flee. The police took her into custody right in front of you and then retrieved the murder weapon not three feet from where she'd been standing."

"In the water. She dropped the knife in the pool."

"Hah! So you admit she was holding it."

Darn. She'd been tricked into that one.

"She was trying to destroy the evidence," Jacobs insisted.

"She was startled by a woman threatening to blow her head off with a shotgun. She'd been out cold, lying on the cement. What do you think she did? Knocked herself out and then carefully laid the knife across her own stomach?"

"Most likely Mrs. Walker sustained her injury during the struggle."

Jennifer leaned forward, refusing to acknowledge such ridiculous logic. "Don't you think Emma Walker is a little too convenient a suspect?"

Jacobs's eyelids dropped until she resembled a cobra. "Are you suggesting that if police find a murder victim with someone standing over them, holding the murder weapon, that their time would be better spent pursuing other suspects? Been watching a little too much TV, Ms. Marsh?"

Not really. Writing too many mysteries maybe. "Look, I don't care what you think happened. I don't even care what I personally saw. What I do know is that Mrs. Emma Walker could not, would not, and did not murder anyone." She hoped.

Jacobs settled back in her chair and studied Jennifer's face. "Your loyalty is admirable. I don't see a lot of loyalty in this job."

Her tone was much softer, but she couldn't fool Jennifer.

"However"—yep, here it came—"your trust in this woman is misplaced. I'm sure it must seem totally unbelievable to you that she could be involved in, let alone commit, such a heinous crime. But let me assure you, I have seen it all, and it is not only possible but highly likely.

No matter what you feel, the fact remains that Edgar Walker is dead. And his murderer is Emma Walker."

The dead part, she'd have to give her. "Whatever happened to a presumption of innocence?"

Jacobs chuckled, one of her mean little laughs.

Hah! She knew Jacobs couldn't keep up that nice person facade for long.

"If Mrs. Walker is so ill-advised as to plead not guilty, she will bring with her a presumption of innocence before her judge and jury."

Jacobs's smile turned sly. "But if I didn't believe she was guilty, I wouldn't be prosecuting her. If, on the off chance, this ever does come to trial, you *will* be called to testify. And you *will* tell the truth. That's all Fulton County asks of you—that you simply tell the truth."

Somehow the truth in this case seemed woefully inadequate.

"Okay, let's abandon the question of guilt for the moment." Jacobs was trying a new tactic. "You say you were at the Walker estate because two of Mrs. Walker's friends called and asked you to check on her."

"One, actually. Mae Belle."

"And how did you gain access to the grounds?"

Definitely a trick question. By telling the truth, she was admitting to entering even if they couldn't get her on the breaking part. But she had to answer the question, and lying was simply not an option. "Two of the fence posts were loose at the bottom. I slipped though."

"And how did you get past the dogs?"

"What dogs?"

"The four trained Dobermans that patrol the grounds every night?"

Jennifer gulped. She'd brought Snausages when it

sounded like what she needed was several pounds of choice T-bones, not to mention full body armor. "The dogs weren't out."

Jacobs seemed a little taken aback. "And the sensors?"

Jennifer shrugged. "I didn't set off anything until I tripped something near the pool."

"So you had free access to the grounds from the fence to the house?"

She nodded. And so had the murderer.

Arlene Jacobs was talking, but Jennifer wasn't hearing a word she was saying. Why wasn't the security system turned on? And why were the dogs kept penned? And this was a big one: Who had turned the sensor back on around the pool once Edgar's body had gone into the water? Because going in, it sure hadn't tripped anything.

Jacobs was right. This real-life crime stuff was actually pretty simple if not downright obvious. Everything was falling neatly into place. Lisa had to have killed Edgar. She was home that night, and she had control of the entire security system. She kept the dogs up. No reason to let their barking interfere with her murdering Edgar. And she'd turned off the system to dump the body in the water after she'd killed him.

Mrs. Walker's presence must have been fortuitous. So Lisa, taking advantage of the situation, had knocked her out, left her at the side of the pool with the murder weapon where she would pick it up when she woke, gone back in the house and turned the pool system back on, and waited. Yes, it all seemed to fit quite nicely. Except for why the rest of the system had been turned off when Mrs. Walker entered the estate earlier, and why she'd been able to gain access several times before without getting caught.

Well, no matter. What didn't fit would be explained in

due time. And as for motive, Jennifer now knew that Edgar wanted a divorce, and Lisa was determined he was not going to get one.

"You'd better take a closer look at Lisa Walker," Jennifer blurted. "With Edgar dead, she has a lot to gain, and she was there that night."

Jacobs looked at Jennifer as if she were drowning in her own confusion. "You can go, Ms. Marsh. I'll see you in court."

Jennifer gathered her purse and headed for the door, throwing one last look in the assistant D.A.'s direction. She could understand Jacobs's wanting to believe Emma was the killer. It made her job a lot easier, and if she herself had been prosecuting this case, she'd probably want to believe it, too.

Jennifer knew she could forget what little hope she'd had that the police would investigate further. The noose was tightening around Emma's neck, and if someone wasn't able to get inside information from the Down Home Grill soon, all hope for Emma was going to disappear.

Maxie Malone was stymied. The fiasco at Rufus's Chocolate Heaven had left her with few options. With the ban in force keeping her from the premises, she had no choice but to pursue other leads. Still, she was sure the key to Rufus Donaldson's death lay at his place of business.

Restlessly, Maxie paced the floor of her apartment. She hadn't heard from the two undercover operatives she'd sent in as hand-dipping chocolate experts. She'd had to go with who was available, and now she was ruing her decision to send in anyone at all. They were a liability—both of them—the petite femme fatale Leandra and the courageous and exotic Teresa. While semicompetent in their own rights, they had no experience with chocolate outside of eating it. They knew even less of subtlety, being more suited to stakeouts and in-your-face confrontations. Yes, their silence was not a good sign, and it was making Maxie more nervous as each hour passed. She would never forgive herself if they wound up as the key ingredients in Rufus's homemade fudge.

Muffy whimpered loudly, lunged, and dropped her food dish in Jennifer's lap.

She picked up the bowl and turned her attention toward

the mutt. "I don't suppose you could wait just five minutes more while I finish this scene?"

Muffy let out a pitiful howl that needed a full moon for proper effect and then collapsed in a defeated heap on the floor.

"All right! Stop your playacting. I know you're overdue for lunch, but I was on a roll. Most dogs don't even get lunch. Your vet would have a fit if she knew I fed you in the middle of the day. She doesn't realize you're really a person. A spoiled person, at that."

She went to the kitchen, scooped up a third of a cup of dry food, and placed it in Muffy's bowl along with a treat. It wasn't enough to make any difference in her diet, but Muffy seemed to believe it was the only thing that kept her from starvation.

Jennifer plopped the bowl down on the floor, Muffy nosing past her and swallowing every morsel in one quick slurp. Jennifer went back to her computer.

Yes, Maxie was becoming concerned. If she didn't hear from her people soon, she'd have no choice but to go in after them.

Jennifer sighed and pushed back from the keyboard. Maxie was worried, but at least Leandra and Teresa both knew martial arts and carried weapons—Teresa a boot knife (she was an expert knife thrower) and Leandra a bolo, being part Australian aborigine. Teri and Leigh Ann, however, were defenseless and not the best improvisers she'd ever met. Most of a week had passed since she'd last talked to them, and their silence was nagging at her. Maybe April had heard something.

She dialed the phone. "April, hi, it's Jen." She hoped none of the tension she was feeling was evident in her voice. She could hear a baby crying in the background.

"What happened?" April sounded more than a little concerned.

"Nothing. I thought maybe you'd heard from Teri or Leigh Ann."

"Oh, my God. They're dead, aren't they?"

April hadn't seemed at all concerned the night they decided to go undercover as waitresses. Jennifer had expected a little reassurance, not a National Emergency Alert.

"No, they're not *dead*. I've just been having a little trouble getting hold of them is all."

"I knew it! They're dead."

A cold sweat broke out on Jennifer's forehead. "They are *not* dead," she insisted, really sorry that she had made the mistake of dragging April into this. "I'll take care of it. Forget I called. 'Bye."

She could hear April gasp even as she dropped the receiver in its cradle. She didn't have much time. She had some shopping to do before she took off for the Down Home Grill.

The floppy denim hat sporting a huge sunflower was pulled snugly over Jennifer's ears and all the way down to her eyebrows. Not a strand of hair was showing, and the blue-tinted lenses of her glasses perfectly hid the color of her eyes. Her face was powdered an adobe brown, her lips brushed with a silvery pink, and a large black beauty mark dotted her left cheek. Her long, shapeless sundress hid the chunky three-inch heels of her boots. If anyone recognized her in that getup, they'd have to be more clever than any sleuth she could dream up.

It was close to six-thirty, but she'd made it to the Down Home Grill as quickly as she could. No matter. Both Teri and Leigh Ann worked the supper shift, even on weekends. If they were still working, she'd know soon enough.

"Malone, party of one," Suzy sang out. "Malone," she repeated, walking straight over to Jennifer, who was leaning against the far wall, staring out the window. "Miss, we have your table ready."

Jennifer nodded, thankful that the red in her makeup was darker than the flush she felt in her cheeks. A good detective would remember her cover name. At least Suzy hadn't recognized her.

"Follow me, please." Suzy led the way, past Teri, who was balancing three platters near the fish tanks, to a small table tucked in the back. Thank goodness she was all right.

"Booth," Jennifer squeaked out in a hoarse whisper.

"Oh, you'd rather have a booth?"

She nodded.

"We usually put our single patrons at the small tables, but we do make exceptions. I know how you feel. I hate those straight-backed chairs, too."

Suzy took her toward the front, where the booths were backed by the large saltwater tank. She waited as Jennifer slid across the slick vinyl and then offered a menu. "Enjoy your meal."

Jennifer ran her eyes over the entrées. Definitely a meat lover's delight. She'd hoped to get away with a bowl of soup, but it looked as if all they had that night was chili and vegetable beef.

"Okay, let's have it. What can I get you?" Teri had snuck up on her, the brim of Jennifer's hat effectively cutting out all of her peripheral vision.

"What's your vegetable of the day?" she asked in the same hoarse voice she'd used on Suzy.

"Green beans cooked with fatback."

Were there no vegetables in this place that hadn't come in contact with some part of an animal?

"Just bring me a baked potato and a tossed salad with honey-mustard dressing."

"Butter and sour cream?"

"No. I want some of that steak sauce to go on it. And a large glass of sweetened tea."

"What kind of steak do you want with that?" Teri asked, impatiently tapping her pen against the order pad.

"No steak, thank you."

"Listen, lady. This is a steak house—"

"Are you this rude to all of your customers, Teri?"

Teri's tapping pencil stopped, and she bent down to stare under the brim of Jennifer's hat. "What the heck are you doing here?"

Jennifer pulled the glasses down to rest on the end of her nose. "Checking on you."

"A bit neurotic, are we? You could have waited until our critique meeting. Leigh Ann and I have every Monday off. Can't miss group." She bent down closer. "You look really, really weird, like you've been shopping in the ethnic section of the cosmetics department. You suffering from pigment envy? You look better as a white girl."

"Nice of you to notice." She scowled and shoved the glasses back into place. "Also nice of you to call me and fill me in once in a while."

"Yeah, well, I've been busy. I got a sample of steak sauce for one of my friends—a grad student at Mercer—to analyze."

"And what'd he find?"

"Nothing. One of his roommates ate it. But I got another sample." She reached in her pocket and let the lid of a small container peek over the edge.

"We don't need to know what's in it," Jennifer told her.

"That's what you think! They act like they've got gold in there, like Fort Knox. Leigh Ann may have found out something about it. She's in the kitchen. They banned her from the floor after the incident with the football players from the University of Georgia. Hot! I mean, those guys could have put out their own calendar."

Hard bodies plus Leigh Ann—not a promising mix. "Was anyone hurt?"

"Heck, no. I got my girl outta there. Only minor scrapes and bruises. I think Roy may be a little sweet on her, 'cause he didn't fire her. If Lisa had been here she'd have had her—"

"Is Lisa here tonight?"

Teri nodded. "In the back somewhere. And if she comes out and sees me talking to you for more than three seconds, she'll have my—"

"All right, already. Just bring me my potato and salad, and don't forget the tea."

Teri stuffed the order pad in her pocket and took off to put in the order.

The rest rooms were not all that far from the kitchen. Jennifer got up and wandered in that direction. She could see Leigh Ann through the opening at the warming bar. She was wearing a large white chef's jacket that had been rolled several times at the sleeves so her hands could peek out, and an enormous chef's hat that came down over her ears and sat precariously on her forehead. She was turning steaks while Gus supervised at her elbow. He leaned forward, said something in her ear, and then it looked as if he was actually nibbling on the lobe. Leigh Ann turned and snapped at him, and her hat slid all the way down her nose, covering both eyes. Gus reached over, pulled the white poof back up, and continued to chat at her in what sounded like Spanish.

Movement caught Jennifer's eye. Through the glass panel of the door in the back of the kitchen that led to the hallway of Edgar's office, she could see Lisa, gesturing wildly. Then she seemed to burst into tears, swiping at her cheeks with the heels of her hands. Whoever she'd been talking with moved in. He was tall, narrow-shouldered, blond with monochromatic coloring, his skin as pale as his hair, and he was folding her to him. Her arm came up and hugged his back. They broke and Jennifer could see them in profile. Benny. Lisa was in the back arguing and making up with Benny. What the heck was *that* all about?

They turned toward the swinging door, and Jennifer ducked back into the dining area, around the fish tank, and into the safety of her booth. The last thing she needed was for Lisa to catch her spying in the restaurant. She slid onto the seat just as the two emerged from the kitchen. Jennifer sat on her knees and peeked through the water to watch them walk to the front door, perfectly businesslike, no hint of the little scene that had played itself out in the back.

"Find anything interesting? There's a baby shark in there. Did you see it?"

Jennifer turned to find Teri sliding her potato and salad across the polyurethane tabletop.

"I hope you plan to leave a tip as if you'd ordered a regular dinner. It's just as much work, you know."

Jennifer plopped herself back down and unwrapped her fork from the paper napkin. "What's with Lisa and Benny?"

"Benny?"

"The blond man with Lisa."

"Oh, him. I don't know. He's in almost every night.

They tell me he's the new manager, but I can't see that he does all that much."

"He and Lisa got something going on?"

"Heck if I know." Teri gave a little shudder. "He gives me the creeps. He's like an albino."

She shook her head. "Blue eyes, not pink. He's just very fair."

"Like I'd know about that."

"Has his sister been in?"

"Carbon copy except for gender, only with some kind of Sixties flower child fixation?"

Jennifer nodded.

"Once. I don't think she and Lisa get along. She spoke maybe two words to her and then took off. She gives me the creeps, too. She looks like a ghost." Teri's eyes kept darting about as if she was afraid Lisa was going to see her spending too much time at Jennifer's table and get suspicious.

"Oh my God—" Teri began.

"What is it?" Jennifer asked, tugging at Teri's sleeve.

But Teri could only stand there, one hand over her open mouth. And then Jennifer saw it, too. Lisa was leading a very regal Monique dressed in a suit and heels, nose well into the air, and an equally decked-out April, to a table in the middle of the restaurant.

Jennifer caught a scrap of the conversation as they passed. ". . . and when do you expect the review to come out, Ms. Dupree?"

Jennifer hung her head. It was bad enough that Leigh Ann was flipping steaks in the kitchen, Teri was slinging food in the dining room, and she was posing as a customer in makeup that made her look ethnically confused. Now

Monique and April were passing themselves off as restaurant critics. She should never have made that call to April.

Monique accepted the menu from Lisa. "You can start us off with an Eddie." Her voice boomed with authority.

"I'll get that for you immediately—and see that your waitress takes good care of you."

Teri stood frozen, but, unfortunately, not invisible. Lisa grabbed her arm and swung her around. "See those two women over there?"

Teri nodded numbly.

"Give them anything they want, and fast. They're reviewing the Grill for the *Atlanta Daily*. I'll alert Gus. You got that?"

Jennifer bowed her head and prayed.

"Now!" Lisa barked.

Teri jumped a little. "Yes, ma'am."

Lisa disappeared without another word.

"Gotta go," Teri said to Jennifer. "I have more *important* customers to wait on."

Jennifer pulled the brim of her hat closer around her face and attacked her baked potato. With any luck, no one else would recognize her.

Now that she'd confirmed that Teri and Leigh Ann were both in good health, if not of sound mind, she was more than ready to get out of the restaurant.

She stole a glance in the direction of Monique's table. Teri was standing there, pointing with her pen, the two women staring straight at her. April smiled and waved, and Jennifer slid as far under the table as she could without actually ducking under it.

Teri scribbled something on her order pad and then walked back to Jennifer's booth. "Why did you tell April that Leigh Ann and I were dead?"

"I did not!"

Teri rolled her eyes and went off toward the kitchen.

She could see April squinting in her direction. No potato, not even one smothered in Edgar's steak sauce, was worth Lisa's wrath. She had to get out of there fast.

She rummaged in her purse and found a ten dollar bill. That should more than cover the cost of her food and Teri's tip. She slid it under her plate and took off toward the front door.

As she pushed through the crowd waiting to be seated, she could see the freedom of the parking lot. But just as her arm touched the push bar on the door, someone's hand closed on her shoulder.

"What the hell are you doing here?" Lisa Walker asked.

Chapter 20

Jennifer froze. She should have broken free, but some-body had filled her legs with sand. As if on auto pilot, she turned. Even towering over Lisa in her three-inch heels, she could feel the woman's power.

"I thought that was you," Lisa said. "We have some talking to do."

The woman grasped her upper arm and led her to the back and through the kitchen. Jennifer thought about calling out for help, but Leigh Ann was too engrossed in her duties at the grill to even notice, not that she'd be much help, all ninety pounds of her. And Gus was still rattling off something in Spanish.

Lisa pushed her through the swinging door into the hall and then on into the office. She let go of her arm and shoved Jennifer into one of the chairs while she took a perch on the side of the desk. She stared straight at Jennifer. Her frown deepened. "What's wrong with your face? Did you get a bad sunburn?"

Jennifer shook her head and stared straight back, right through the blue of her glasses. She wasn't about to let Lisa throw her off with criticism. She knew all about those tactics. She'd had parents.

Just let her make a move. She was ready for anything

Lisa had to dish out—even if Lisa did have a good thirty pounds on her, all of it muscle.

"I spoke with Arlene Jacobs. She tells me you think I killed my husband."

Oh, this was just great. She was trapped in the back of a noisy restaurant with a killer who was most likely going to confess her crimes and then try to do her in like she had Edgar.

Lisa probably planned to chop her up and make barbecue like they did in *Fried Green Tomatoes*. Well, she was as well-read as anyone, and she was not about to let Lisa outdo her. She rummaged in her purse, and her hand closed on what she was searching for. She'd once read an article titled "101 Ways to Defend Yourself with a Ballpoint Pen." Hah! Let Lisa come after her now.

But Lisa dropped her eyes, tucked her bleached hair behind her ears, and licked her lips. For a moment she looked sad, not menacing, like she'd been through a lot. This murder business must be taking a toll.

When she raised her eyes, they were again full of fury. "I didn't kill Edgar," she said, her voice harsh and strong, "and you have no right to suggest to anyone that I did. You may not believe it, but I loved him."

Yeah, right. Hard-as-nails Lisa was hardly her idea of the grieving widow, and it hadn't been fifteen minutes since she'd seen her in the arms of another man.

Lisa hugged herself and half turned away. Was she actually crying? Boy, she was good. Quite a convincing actress and quite a different persona from the one that went with the netted midriff minidress and boots she had on.

"Go on," Jennifer said, curious what this black widow was going to come up with next.

"I don't feel sorry for Emma, and I won't let her get away with killing Edgar. She took my life away."

Lisa's voice broke, and Jennifer felt a tear well in her own eye. She blinked it away and silently chastised herself. Movies, puppies, babies, TV commercials, even greeting cards made her cry. Her reaction was no proof of Lisa's innocence.

"Why are you telling me this?"

"I know you're her friend, but Emma didn't love Edgar. When he died, I lost someone I cared for deeply, and I won't be robbed again by someone trying to defend his murderer." A hard edge had returned to her voice. Jennifer's hand tightened around the pen.

For a moment she had almost believed her, almost swallowed that the woman might have found something in ol' Edgar that rang her bell, but she'd laid it on an inch too thick. This had to be an act. No one could love Edgar Walker like that. Could they? Besides, Lisa didn't know she knew about Benny.

"Is that it?" Jennifer asked.

"That's it."

"Can I go now?"

Lisa nodded. "But remember this: you don't know me. I may not be who you think I am."

If Lisa were even half of who Jennifer thought she was, she'd do well to get out of that office fast.

"I can't find her." Sam's voice resonated across the phone line as Jennifer finished the last bite of her lunch, sliced red pepper and cheese on toast with potato chips. He sounded out of breath.

"I know that. I was with you when you went to Natalie's apartment, remember?" Jennifer let out an exasperated sigh as she popped the last chip into her mouth. Even the mention of the woman sent her blood pressure flying.

"No, I mean I can't find a record of her. I'm calling from Emory. I checked with their alumni office. The only Natalie Brewster they have listed over the last decade died in a car accident three years ago."

The potato chip stuck in her throat. She had read about this sort of thing happening. She'd even written about it in her Jolene Arizona novel, but she'd never come face-to-face with it in real life. It sent goose bumps dancing up her arms. She held the phone in the crook of her neck as she shoved her tray onto the coffee table, brushed off her hands, and swallowed hard.

"Let me guess. The deceased received an MBA and, had she lived, would now be in her late twenties. Were you able to get a description of her?"

"Yeah. Medium height, dark hair, green eyes."

The green eyes should have been the giveaway. She could kick herself for letting it get past her. "How green were Natalie's eyes?"

"Bright. Emerald."

"Artificial."

"You think?"

"Only in books do people have eyes that color. They had to be contact lenses. I don't suppose you bothered to look for that telltale ring on the iris." She didn't wait for an answer. She knew he hadn't. "Her hair was probably dyed, too."

For a moment neither of them spoke. She knew he was kicking himself, too. And probably mourning the loss of a beautiful creature that never was.

They needn't bother checking out the rest of her résumé. Phony name, phony degree. Why would she sprinkle it with truth? Even her physical description was all wrong. She could easily have had help with that perfect figure, too.

"Where'd Edgar do his banking?" Her throat constricted around the words.

"We'll have to get a release to look at the records."

"Call Emma. She still owns most of the business. She can give you the go-ahead."

"Right," he said.

The phone clicked and began to hum in her ear. She let the receiver fall into its cradle.

Jennifer's mind was racing ahead. Maybe this had all been a mistake. Maybe the alumni office at Emory had made some kind of error, and Natalie Brewster wasn't the scheming, swindling thief that Jennifer's mind was rushing to make her out. Maybe she was all wrong.

Sure, and maybe she was a bestselling author.

Leigh Ann moaned from somewhere amid the stack of throw pillows piled on the corner unit of Monique's sofa.

"Would someone just shoot that girl and put her out of her misery?" Teri asked. "I'm tired of listening to her whine."

It was a tempting suggestion.

"Why don't you quit?" Jennifer asked. It'd be a relief not having to worry about whether or not these two were safe. "I can't see that you're getting much of anywhere, anyway."

Leigh Ann dug her way out through the pile of chintz. "Not getting anywhere? Excuse me?"

The effort must have been too much for her. She collapsed back on top of the pillows.

"The girls seem to be doing fine," April observed. "You didn't have to call me up and terrify me into going down there." She munched on a carrot stick. At least it was healthier than the square of fudge she'd just finished.

"That was a misunderstanding. I never said—"

"Enough!" Monique had stopped rocking. "If anyone has anything to report, I suggest they do it now, so we can get on with this meeting. Teri?"

"Lisa is the main man. I mean that girl really hustles." Teri lay flat on the floor on her stomach apparently too tired to flex a muscle.

"I thought Roy—" Jennifer began.

"Ah, Roy . . ." Leigh Ann purred from her pillow fortress.

"Roy knows what's what," Teri went on, "but Lisa's got it in line. That girl has her eye on everything and everybody. If there's a problem, she's right there. I've even seen her wait tables when things got really out of hand. She has one of those photographic memories. Doesn't even write down an order."

"Yeah, and it drives Gus nuts, too," Leigh Ann said. She rolled over on her side, her chin propped on her hand. "I don't know if you've noticed, but she has the most incredible clothes."

Incredible was one word. At least Lisa had the most expensive bad taste money could buy.

"Have you ever seen anything that might suggest that Lisa and Roy might have something going on?" Jennifer asked. She couldn't see whatever it was that had both Suzy and Leigh Ann gaga over this guy. He couldn't sing and he wielded one heck of a frying pan. Okay. Strike the Leigh Ann part. The fact that Roy was male was probably sufficient to explain *her* interest. But Lisa did dress like a flirt, and Roy seemed to get around.

Leigh Ann started to giggle. "You're not suggesting incest, now are you?"

Her words left Jennifer practically speechless. "What?" she managed.

"Silly, I thought you knew. Lisa and Roy are first cousins."

"Get outta here!" Teri raised up and slapped at Leigh Ann's knee. "They sure don't act like kin, but now that you mention it, they do have a similar body type, kind of round all over."

"How'd you find out?" Jennifer asked.

"He told me. Guess he didn't want me getting jealous. One of the other gals who works there is after him hot and heavy."

She had to mean Suzy.

"But I don't think he's interested in her," Leigh Ann went on.

This whole conversation was descending into *Days of Our Lives at the Down Home Grill*. Monique had begun tapping her foot. Not a good sign.

Jennifer jerked to attention. "Anything else?"

"Well, I did hear one thing," Teri volunteered. "Two days before old man Walker was murdered, some woman who works there but doesn't really work there—"

"Yeah, I've heard about her," Leigh Ann interrupted. "She's supposed to be God's gift to men."

"Yeah, that's the one. Anyway, she brought in a couple of guys, one wearing a Rolex, the other one of those diamond pinky rings, to look the place over right at the height of the supper rush."

"Franchisees," Jennifer said, more to herself than anyone else.

"Is that a word?" Leigh Ann asked.

"Yeah, look it up," Jennifer said. "I'd expect Natalie Brewster had a parade of these potential franchisees through the place."

"Maybe," Teri continued. "But after that day, she never came back, and no one's seen her since."

Disappeared. Like the woman in that old joke who took off her wig, her dentures, her false eyelashes, her contact lenses—and she wasn't there anymore.

Chapter 21

"But she's my sister." Jennifer hiccuped between big gulps that were supposed to simulate sobs. She didn't do well with lying, although she should be getting better at it. She'd certainly had enough practice. She hoped God had a special clause for people trying to help unjustly accused little old ladies, because otherwise she'd have some serious explaining to do when she met St. Peter.

Sam leaned over and awkwardly put his arm about her, the bucket seat of her Volkswagen getting in the way. The pen in his sports jacket pocket dug painfully into her shoulder.

"You'll have to excuse my wife. She's very upset," he told the man in the guard house.

Jennifer stiffened. When they'd decided to pull this con on the second-shift security officer at Natalie Brewster's apartment complex, nothing had been mentioned about their pretending to be married. Marriage was not something to be taken lightly. It was serious stuff, and while the notion that someday something might happen between the two of them had not escaped her . . .

Sam nudged her waist. He was staring gravely at the guard and, she supposed, waiting for her to make her next brilliant move. Fine, then. She would.

She stopped hiccuping and went straight for the kill. Dry-eyed, she looked unflinchingly at the security guard and raised one eyebrow. People threatening to sue always raised one eyebrow. It was to signal that she had an ace in the hole, and he'd better think twice before refusing to let her into the complex. "My sister suffers from grand mal epilepsy, and I haven't been able to get her on the phone for over a week. If—"

"Okay. Go to the office. It's down the first right. Tell Hilda I said to let you in, but you'll have to sign a waiver."

She flashed him a smile and floored the gas pedal of the Beetle. It puttered forward.

She shrugged out of Sam's arm. "Married?"

"I had to tell him something. It seemed reasonable."

Not to her. At least not yet. She grumbled and took the first right.

Most of the lot in front of the office was empty. Few people were home at four in the afternoon, and the resident manager was more than happy to be of help.

"Now calm down," the older woman soothed, turning the key in the lock of Brewster's apartment. She looked like the housemother of a sorority. Plump, friendly. "My mother always said, 'Don't worry before it's time.' Your sister is probably just fine. I had no idea she suffered from anything serious," she confessed. "Such a perfectly beautiful young woman. You wouldn't think—"

"Yeah, you wouldn't," Jennifer cut her off short, adjusting her shoulder bag. She felt Sam's hand on her arm.

"My wife's a bit on edge," Sam explained.

And she was going to get a bit more on edge if he didn't cut out this wife bit.

"And she has every reason to be," the older woman observed. "Family has to watch out for family. One of my sisters went missing once for three days. When she came home, she told us she hadn't been lost. Said she knew exactly where she was every minute, which, I suppose, is one way to look at it. I suspect your sister knows where she is, too. Of course, mine didn't have a medical condition."

The woman took a deep breath and pushed open the door. Obviously afraid of what might lie inside, she let Jennifer and Sam go in first.

It looked like one of those ads for furniture stores that come in the Sunday newspaper. White sofa and love seat, glass end table and coffee table, matching lamps, airy rattan dinette set. Tasteful, pleasant, but something seemed wrong.

Quickly, Jennifer's eyes darted about the room. Suddenly, it struck her. It wasn't what was there, but rather what wasn't. Not a personal item in sight. No TV. No stereo. No photos, throw pillows, mail, keys, books, or jewelry. Nothing on the walls. Nothing anywhere. The place was completely sterile.

"Neat, isn't she?" Hilda observed.

"Too neat," Sam muttered.

Jennifer jabbed him with her elbow and then clutched his sleeve. "I need some water," she croaked. He led her into the small kitchen cubicle. No toaster—an absolute necessity of life—and no microwave. Only a lone two-cup coffeemaker and a single roll of paper towels.

Quickly and silently, Jennifer opened and closed cabinets and drawers. Everything was empty. She then peered in the cabinet over the sink. Two tumblers, two mugs, spoons, a small canister of coffee, a creamer, and some sugar packets.

Sam turned the faucet on loudly while Jennifer dug a pen from her purse and managed, with a paper towel, to slip the glassware off the shelf, wrap it, and secrete it in her purse.

"They look like they're clean. I doubt we'll find any fingerprints," he whispered.

"Someone put them in the cabinet," she insisted. "We need a look at the bedroom," she added.

They joined Hilda in the living room as she was drawing back the drapes and opening the sliding glass door to a small balcony. "This place still has the smell of paint."

"When did this complex open?" Sam asked.

"About six months ago. Your wife's sister was one of our first tenants."

"I was afraid her rent might be overdue," Jennifer suggested.

"Oh, no, dear. Miss Brewster paid in cash up front for the term of her lease. She still has a good while before she owes us anything."

Jennifer nodded at a closed door. "Is that the bedroom?"

"Yes," Hilda assured her. "This is our smallest unit, basically three rooms with a bath, but high quality."

Jennifer opened the door a crack and let out a squeak. Quickly, she pulled it shut. Hilda could not be allowed inside that room. She might start asking questions, and Jennifer was fresh out of answers. She turned, bumping into Sam, who was at her shoulder.

"I'm not feeling well. I wonder if I could lie down. Alone. I'm a little dizzy."

Sam frowned, apparently confused. But Hilda was coming up fast from behind. He turned and, taking the woman's elbow, led her back toward the sofa.

"Let's give her a moment." He nodded in Jennifer's direction. "Morning sickness. You know how it is."

"Oh, really? Even this late in the day?" Hilda asked.

"Morning, noon, evening. Sometimes in the middle of

the night . . ." she could hear Sam saying as she closed the door behind her.

That man. Not only did he have them married, now he had her pregnant. Well, she wasn't about to let him drag Jaimie into this or into her thoughts. She had work to do. She had to find something, anything, that might help her clear Mrs. Walker, but it sure didn't look like she was going to find it here.

Jennifer scanned the bedroom. Except for the light gray carpeting and miniblinds on the windows, it was totally empty, not even an indentation from a furniture leg.

Quickly, she crossed to the bathroom. It, too, was empty except for a roll of toilet paper and another roll of paper towels. Not even a shower curtain. She pulled open the medicine cabinet. Empty.

Well, if Natalie Brewster had stood in that bathroom with her long, dark hair for even a minute, she almost certainly had left something behind.

Jennifer tore off a paper towel, got down on her hands and knees, and ran it over the linoleum. Sure enough, when she turned over the towel, gathered with the dust were two long, dark strands of hair.

A sharp thud sounded on the bedroom door. "You all right in there?" Sam's muffled voice called. "Hilda's getting concerned about you. She wants to come in and check on you."

Quickly, Jennifer rolled the towel into a tight ball and stuffed it in her bag. She scooted to the bedroom door, opened it a crack, and slipped through into the living room.

". . . water weight gain. Of course. But don't have that ring resized yet. You'll just have to have it redone again later. It doesn't really matter if she wears one or not unless it makes her too self-conscious once she starts to show," Hilda was saying.

"Oh, dear. You look a bit flushed," Hilda went on, catching sight of Jennifer's face. "You sure you're all right?"

"Perfect," Jennifer assured her. "Sis must be fine, too. Probably on a business trip. She takes those sometimes. Must have forgotten to tell me."

Hilda was smiling broadly. "Your husband was explaining to me why you don't wear your wedding band and about your mood swings. Hormones will do that to you, honey, especially when you've got a bun in the oven."

She'd stepped out of the room for two seconds to do some real detective work, and Sam had accused her of mood swings. From a bun in the oven. As if she needed an excuse. She'd be as moody as she pleased, anytime she pleased, thank you, and she didn't need to be pregnant to do it.

She grinned and pecked him on the cheek, her nails digging deep into the crook of his arm. "Isn't he a gem?" she asked through clenched teeth. "Well, we must run. Doctor's appointment. Amniocentesis. His family carries some ghastly disorders." She shook her head. "Shouldn't be allowed to breed, actually, but by the time I found out, it was too—"

"Thanks for your time, Hilda." Sam was shaking the woman's hand as he shuffled her out the door.

Hilda was looking more than a little confused. "Right." They left her standing, bewildered, on the apartment building steps.

Jennifer carefully laid her purse in the backseat and then jumped behind the steering wheel of her car. Sam was almost as quick. He pulled on his seat belt as Jennifer took off as quickly as the Bug would go toward the gate.

"Genetic disorders?"

"You're the one who made me pregnant." She stopped short. "Figuratively, of course. And gave me bloating. *And* mood swings."

"Yeah. That last one was a stretch."

She gunned the engine.

"Is that why you're so angry?"

"No. I'm upset because Natalie Brewster brought you here, to this apartment, and you didn't even notice she wasn't living here." She took one more look in her rearview mirror at Hilda, who was still transfixed on the spot.

"What'd you find in the bedroom?"

"Carpet. How could you let her get this past you?"

"She served me coffee. We worked at the table. She had papers that looked legit. Why should I be suspicious?"

She scowled at him. If he'd been looking at anything other than Natalie, he *would* have noticed.

"Okay. Don't answer that. I goofed up. I guess I thought she was new in town."

This time she growled. "Yeah, new in town with enough money to pay a year's lease worth of rent up front. Any news on the bank records?"

"Not yet. I'm still working on it."

Somehow, they had to find this Natalie Brewster, for lack of a better name to call her. She had managed to worm her way into Edgar Walker's confidence and the confidence of all the people involved with his plans to franchise. But she couldn't have done it alone. She had to have had help. If Jennifer remembered correctly, Mrs. Walker had mentioned something about Edgar's attorney, Walter Ornsby, introducing the two of them. If anyone knew who this mystery woman was, it had to be Ornsby.

Chapter 22

Walter Ornsby, Southern gentleman and semiretired attorney at law, had some explaining to do, and Jennifer wasn't about to wait to make another trip to Atlanta so he could do it.

"Don't you want to get a bite to eat before we barge in?" Sam asked in the elevator of O'Hara's Tara.

Sam was used to missing meals, so what was his problem? They could get something on their way home. All she wanted right now were some answers.

"It'd give you a minute to sit down, relax . . ."

He didn't add "cool off," which, she had to admit, was to his credit. Still, she refused to speak. She didn't want to get into another argument right now, and she couldn't think of a single remark that wouldn't start one. She was still smarting from the curve he'd thrown her at Natalie's apartment building. It was bad enough that he'd told Hilda they were married. He didn't have to make her pregnant, too. Bringing a child like Jaimie into this world was far too important a responsibility to be treated so lightly.

"You used pregnancy before in a disguise," he reminded her, apparently not smart enough to just let it go.

"No, I did not. I used a towel to make myself look fat. It's not my fault other people thought I was—"

141

"Okay, okay. No more about any of this. Next time you're suddenly taken ill, I'll say it was food poisoning."

"And nothing about mood swings," she added.

"Got it," Sam agreed. "One more thing. Who is this Jaimie you were muttering about in the car on the way over here?"

"Jaimie?" she asked, wincing. People weren't supposed to listen to mutterings. If they weren't private, the mutterer would say them out loud.

"Yeah. Jaimie."

There was no way she could explain to Sam that she had established a relationship with the egg that was to become her firstborn child. Actually named it. Men didn't understand these things. Heck, nobody who wasn't female, pushing thirty, and definitely on the wrong side of neurotic, could possibly—

The elevator door popped open, and Jennifer led the way down the hall. She found the apartment near the end and pressed the bell.

"You were about to tell me about Jaimie—"

"No, I wasn't. Now just act normal," she told him, giving him a quick once-over and straightening his tie. "Let me do the—"

The door came open and Ornsby's immaculately groomed and handsomely thin self was looking at them as if they'd rung the wrong bell. "Yes?" he asked, belting a smoking jacket over his dress shirt and slacks.

Jennifer offered her hand. "We met at Emma Walker's."

"Oh, yes, Miss Marsh." Ornsby accepted her hand. "And . . ."

Sam reached across Jennifer and the two men shook. "Sam Culpepper."

"Of course. I remember. Won't you come in?"

Jennifer brushed past the man and down the hallway. His condo was a carbon copy of Mrs. Walker's, the most expensive model, the one with a view.

She sat on a dark green leather sofa. The place was decorated with a hunt motif. Sam joined her.

From a mahogany end table, Ornsby selected a meerschaum pipe carved in the shape of a wood sprite, filled the bowl from a canister of sweet-smelling tobacco, and settled into a wing chair. "May I offer you some coffee or perhaps a brandy?"

Jennifer shook her head. "Who is Natalie Brewster?" she asked, she hoped, politely. After all, the man was supposed to be on their side. He *was* Mrs. Walker's attorney. She shouldn't have to tiptoe around him.

Ornsby flicked open a silver lighter, brought it near the pipe and drew hard on the stem. The flame dipped into the bowl, and small puffs of smoke escaped his mouth. She had a feeling nothing hurried this man.

He stared at her from under his full eyebrows, and then spoke to Sam. "Would you care to explain the nature of this inquiry?"

Definitely old school. She knew there was something about the man she hadn't liked.

Sam leaned forward. "We're talking to some of the people Edgar Walker was working with, trying to get an idea of what was going on at the restaurant, who might have had a grudge against him."

Ornsby continued to puff on his pipe as though studying the two of them. He had a smug expression on his face. "I see. And you think that you are likely to uncover some pertinent fact that Mr. Larue and Mr. Heckemyer might overlook?"

Jennifer didn't share Ornsby's confidence in the old

boy network, and she'd had just about all the male chauvinist behavior she intended to tolerate, elder or no. She slipped forward on the sofa. "Who *is* Natalie Brewster?" she repeated.

"Emma told Jennifer that you recommended Ms. Brewster as a consultant to Edgar Walker," Sam explained.

"Why, yes. Miss Brewster has excellent qualifications. I reviewed her résumé. She's well-trained, experienced—"

"She's dead," Jennifer finished.

Ornsby breathed deeply, filling his lungs with smoke, and looked straight at her. He was irritatingly calm. He held the smoke for several seconds and then blew it out. Pipe smokers who inhaled were asking for the worst kind of trouble. But then maybe Walter Ornsby liked living dangerously.

"When did this happen?" he asked.

"Three years ago," Sam said.

Ornsby pursed his lips. He looked almost relieved, but whatever he was feeling, he was covering it well. He rested the pipe in a glass ashtray. "Obviously we are speaking about two different—"

"That's right," Jennifer jumped in, aware of how hostile she sounded but unable to do anything about it. Maybe Sam had been right. She should have waited, had something to eat, calmed down. Because right now she was feeling aggressive, and she had no time for games. "The woman you introduced to Edgar Walker is not the woman who earned a master's in business administration from Emory University."

Sam's hand was on her arm, warning.

"I knew Miss Brewster's parents. She contacted me, asked me to make the introduction." The older man's words were calm and measured. "I assure you, Miss

Marsh, that at my age I have a tendency to take people at face value. How do I know you are who you say you are? I have asked for no identification, and you have offered none. Yet, were someone to come to my door right now, I would not hesitate to introduce you as Jennifer Marsh. If this child who called herself Natalie Brewster misrepresented herself to me, I can only say that it was in good faith that I perpetuated that fraud."

It sounded reasonable enough. And why shouldn't she believe him—other than the fact that he was a lawyer and had agreed that Emma should plead guilty? Okay, so she didn't believe him, but he didn't have to know that. She let out a breath and forced herself to sound more relaxed.

"I'm sorry if we've been rude," she said, looking him straight in the eyes. "I've been—"

"Distraught, obviously," Ornsby finished. "We all have." He smiled for the first time. "Would you like that brandy now?"

She shook her head. She never drank except for a glass of wine now and then. Brandy was way out of her league, and she needed her wits about her.

"Well, then, if there's nothing else . . ."

Sam was half on his feet when she tugged him back down.

"One more thing," she said. She had to get this interview over with. She didn't think she'd have the courage to confront him again. "You drew up Edgar's will, and you probated it upon his death. Who are his heirs?"

"It was very simple. Edgar left most everything to Lisa."

"But he was paying alimony to Emma—"

"Only a small stipend. I believe Emma viewed it more as Edgar's monthly penance. She certainly didn't need the money. She made more from the business than he did,"

Ornsby assured her, "and then she has the inheritance from her family. One can only spend so much."

She wouldn't know. She always ran out of money before she ran out of spending.

"What about Babs and Benny?"

"Edgar did leave each of them his interest in the restaurants they manage."

"Anything else?"

"Only a small trust fund to one Melissa Bordeaux of Lorraine."

Chapter 23

Maxie Malone frowned at the distinguished white-haired man, his mustache neatly trimmed, sitting behind the desk in the office of his law practice. He'd been dancing around her questions for the last ten minutes. She'd like to grab him by the throat, or better yet, the ends of that mustache, and shake that self-satisfied expression right off his face. What she'd come to ask him was a matter of public record, but she wanted to hear it now, from his own lips. Who had Rufus left his money to?

"All right, Ms. Malone, I'll tell you," Walt Bigsby assured her, drawing on his big cigar. "Rufus Donaldson's heirs included his current wife Lorelei, his first wife's nephews, and his second wife's great-aunt."

His second wife's great-aunt?

Jennifer tapped lightly on the keyboard before pressing the save button. She rubbed the back of her neck. How'd that aunt get mixed up in all of this? The same way that Melissa Bordeaux had gotten herself into Edgar Walker's will.

It was late—close to eleven—and she'd forgotten to eat supper—again. Maybe there were still some of those little chocolate-covered doughnuts she'd bought at Kroger's the other day. Now that they'd come to mind, she wouldn't stop thinking about them until she ate one.

She went to the kitchen. Sure enough, there were four left. She might as well finish them off. She wouldn't want them to get stale.

When she opened the refrigerator door to pour a glass of milk, Muffy bounded from her spot on the rug and skittered to a stop, with her nose poking in at the deli bin. As if Jennifer were going to slice cheese just for her.

"Not this time, Muff." She kneed the dog out of the way, closed the door, and carried her milk and doughnuts back to the couch. She settled down with her feet on the coffee table, eating directly from the box. Mmmmmm. The heck with gold. The streets of Heaven must be paved with chocolate.

A loud knock hit her apartment door, followed by a slam made by what sounded like an open palm. "Open up! Jen, let me in!"

Jennifer stopped chewing as Muffy broke into a barking/dancing frenzy. The voice sounded like Leigh Ann's, but what the heck—

"If she kills me, my blood will be on your hands!"

Jennifer swallowed the bite of doughnut whole. In less than two seconds she had the door unbolted. Leigh Ann, who was dressed in her oversized chef's jacket, practically fell into her arms.

"Just get me inside," she croaked.

Quickly, Jennifer slammed the door and threw both the dead bolt and the regular lock. Before she was able to get the chain on, another loud thump shook the entry. Jennifer jumped and then looked through the peephole.

Suzy's young face, distorted almost beyond recognition,

stared back at her. She was beyond angry. She looked homicidal.

"I know you're in there, Leigh Ellen. Now open this door before I have to get really tough." Each word was emphasized with a thump of her small fist.

Muffy whined and slunk back toward the coffee table.

Jennifer turned to glare at Leigh Ann, her jaw clenched so hard her teeth ached.

"That crazy woman followed me all the way from Atlanta—chased me right out of the restaurant. I thought I'd lost her near Forsyth when I slipped off the interstate and then back on again. But dang if she didn't show back up in my rearview mirror. And then I—"

"All right!" If Leigh Ann wasn't careful, she might find as much danger on this side of the door as she would in the hall. "What did you do?"

"Let me in! I'm not leaving before you talk to me," Suzy hollered through the door.

"If she keeps that racket up, one of my neighbors is going to call 911," Jennifer warned.

Leigh Ann peeped through the viewer, jerking back as another slam rocked the door. "But you can't—"

"Over there," Jennifer ordered, pointing to the couch.

Meekly, Leigh Ann backed to the sofa.

"Sit!" Jennifer ordered.

Both Muffy and Leigh Ann obeyed.

Jennifer turned back to the door, unbolting it.

"Don't!" Leigh Ann shrieked as Jennifer threw open the door, blocking the entryway with her body.

"Miss Marsh? What are *you* doing here?" Suzy gasped in surprise. "I thought—"

Jennifer pulled her inside and slammed the door.

Just then Suzy caught sight of Leigh Ann and lunged, but

Jennifer took hold of her around the waist as she strained toward the petite brunette, who was again on her feet.

"You, down," she ordered. Leigh Ann and Muffy slipped back into their places.

"You, too." She dumped Suzy in one of the upholstered chairs. Suzy reared up but Jennifer kept an arm on her shoulder.

"Now what the heck is going on here?" Jennifer demanded.

"She—she—she—" Suzy dissolved into tears, crying like a three-year-old who'd had her favorite toy swiped by some other kid.

Jennifer slipped onto the chair arm and cradled the young woman as Suzy sobbed loudly on her shoulder, soaking the cotton of her blouse. Muffy crawled on her belly to Jennifer's feet and lay whimpering.

Leigh Ann sat forward and tentatively reached out a hand in Suzy's direction.

Jennifer frowned and shook her head. Not good to pet an injured animal, particularly when she was the one who had caused the injury.

"There now," Jennifer soothed, stroking Suzy's hair. "Tell me what happened."

"Roy asked *her* to the Mayfield family reunion." Suzy let out a wail, collapsed back against Jennifer, and began hyperventilating.

"Quit that," Jennifer ordered, "or you'll pass out." But Suzy continued to draw great, noisy breaths.

"I didn't realize she was so—" Leigh Ann began.

"Well, she is," Jennifer snapped.

Suzy gulped. "Do you realize what this means?" she asked.

Jennifer nodded and continued to stroke her hair.

"No one takes a date to a family reunion unless . . . unless they're as good as engaged." Suzy whined and collapsed again against Jennifer's shoulder. "Me and Roy," she managed between sobs, "we were pre-engaged."

Again Jennifer glared at Leigh Ann. All she was supposed to do was gather a little information, not break this young girl's heart.

Leigh Ann looked like she'd been knocked silly, her lips parted as if in shock. She shook her head and closed her mouth. "I had no idea."

"And you wouldn't have cared if you did," Suzy choked out.

Leigh Ann drew herself up. "Of course I care."

Suzy rubbed the tears from her eyes, cleared her throat and sat up. "You do?"

Leigh Ann licked her lips. "Gee, Suzy, I'm sorry. I didn't know the two of you were so serious."

Suzy squeaked. "I don't know about Roy anymore, but I know I am."

Suddenly, Suzy's eyes darted back and forth between Jennifer and Leigh Ann. She pulled away. "How is it you came to be in Leigh Ellen's apartment?" she asked Jennifer. "Do the two of you *know* each other?"

At that moment Jennifer wished she could deny any involvement whatsoever with Leigh Ann, but that wouldn't be fair to either Suzy or her friend. Leigh Ann was at the restaurant for only one reason—to help *her* out. If anyone bore any responsibility for Suzy's suffering, it was her.

"This is my apartment, Suzy."

"Yours?"

Jennifer nodded.

"But, Miss Marsh, why would—"

There wasn't anything to do but tell the poor girl the

truth. "Leigh Ann is helping me find out who really killed Edgar Walker."

"You mean she's not—"

"That's right. I'm not really a chef's assistant," Leigh Ann confessed.

"I already knew that," Suzy said. "Anyone could tell—"

"And Leigh Ann's not actually in love with Roy. It was all part of an act," Jennifer said emphatically.

Leigh Ann's eyes grew wide, a pained expression on her face. "But—"

"Isn't that right, Leigh Ann?" Jennifer added, her eyes dangerously narrow, her chin pointing toward Suzy, who was staring open-mouthed at her rival.

"Then you mean she's not going to take Roy away from me?"

Leigh Ann cleared her throat. "Heck, no. I was just trying to—"

"Gather information," Jennifer finished. "You know that Emma Walker has been charged with Edgar's murder."

"Of course I do. That's all anyone at the restaurant talked about the week it happened. And it's been on every newscast in Atlanta, or so I've been told. I don't watch a lot of news myself," Suzy confessed.

"Well, what you don't know is that Emma Walker is innocent."

"Oh, I get it!" All her tears were dried up now, and Jennifer could almost see the wheels whirling as Suzy put two and two together. "You're like private eyes!" She clapped her hands together and started bouncing up and down on the chair cushion. "This is so exciting! You know, I knew right from the start that sweet little old lady could never have killed that yucky old man."

Jennifer couldn't have put it better herself.

"So what can I do to help?" Suzy asked.

Jennifer sighed. She hadn't intended to recruit Suzy, but what the heck. No doubt she would be a better source of information than either Leigh Ann or Teri, both of whom had trouble distinguishing reality from the fiction they wrote. And who knew what Suzy might have picked up in the weeks prior to Edgar's death?

"If you do help us, you have to keep it a secret," Jennifer insisted.

"Even from Roy?" Suzy asked.

"Especially from Roy."

"But he needs to know—" Suzy pointed at Leigh Ann.

"That's all right. Trust me. We won't have to tell him a thing. Leigh Ann will simply cease to have anything more to do with him." Jennifer was staring straight at Leigh Ann, who was opening and closing her mouth as if wanting to say something but knowing she didn't dare. "Isn't that right, Leigh Ann?"

Leigh Ann settled for a twist of the head that finally settled into a nod.

"Okay, now both Teri and Leigh Ann—" Jennifer began.

"You mean that other new girl was in on this, too?" Suzy interrupted, her eyes even wider.

Jennifer nodded.

Suzy seemed to think for a moment, and then said shyly, "I hate to say anything against any of Roy's kinfolk, but if I had to guess from everybody working at the restaurant who might have killed Mr. Walker, I'd have to say it was Lisa. She can be downright scary."

At least they were on the same wavelength. "Okay. Let's say that Lisa did kill her husband. You told me when we had breakfast together that Edgar wanted a divorce, that Louise had overheard them fighting about it. Why?"

Suzy tapped her index finger to her bottom lip. "Lisa's pretty hard to get along with, and he wasn't no jewel himself, but Mr. Walker was in love with someone else. And I think I finally figured out who."

Jennifer leaned forward. This was too good to be true. "Who?" she asked, hoping beyond hope that Suzy was about to give them the name that would crack this case wide open.

Suzy took a deep breath and blinked hard. "I'm surprised she didn't tell you. Edgar was still in love with Emma."

Chapter 24

"Emma?" Jennifer repeated, drawing back as if she'd been hit by a two-by-four. She had no idea who she'd expected Suzy to name, but Emma hadn't made the first hundred. "He couldn't possibly—"

"Don't underestimate the power of true love," Suzy insisted. "Once you fall hard for somebody and choose to spend as many years together as those two did, it's hard to let go. Me and Roy have only been together six months, but I can't imagine living without him."

"But what," other than the stars in her eyes, "would make you think that Edgar still loved Emma?"

"For one thing, he kept her picture in his wallet. I saw it one time when he gave me some money to run a personal errand for him. It was an old snapshot. She was a real cutie back then—when it was made. Looked just like she does now only lots younger. And with less wrinkles."

Sentimentality could easily explain the photo. "Keeping someone's picture in your wallet is hardly enough to—"

"I don't know," Leigh Ann jumped in. "He had to be taking a big risk with Lisa, carrying something like that around. I know if one of my boyfriends had his ex in his wallet . . ."

Jennifer shook her head. "It's not enough."

"Okay, then, how about a phone call begging her to meet him at his house late at night?" Suzy offered.

"When?"

"Several months ago, Roy sent me back to Mr. Walker's office to get a check for a delivery we'd just received. The door was open, and Mr. Walker was standing there talking on the phone, his back to me. I guess he didn't hear me come in, and I didn't want to disturb his conversation. I didn't mean to listen. It sort of just happened."

"And he was talking to Emma?" Jennifer asked.

Suzy nodded. "They set up a time—midnight—to meet. He said at the house. I thought it was really weird, eerielike, meeting at the witching hour. That's why I remember it."

"How do you know for sure who he was talking to?"

"He called her Emma, plain as day."

"That still doesn't mean anything was going on between them."

Suzy was trying to help, Jennifer was sure, but this latest revelation, while having some implications for Lisa, was even more damning to Mrs. Walker's case. Had Emma actually been meeting Edgar in the middle of the night? Was all that talk of pranks only a cover? She took a deep breath. Had Emma been lying to her?

"Don't say anything about that phone conversation to anyone," Jennifer warned.

"Okay," Suzy agreed, looking a little taken aback. "It's not like anyone was asking me about it anyway."

Jennifer glanced at her watch. It was close to twelve. "The two of you had better head home," she suggested. "Suzy, you have to drive all the way back to Atlanta, and Leigh Ann has her regular day job to go to before she and Teri—"

Leigh Ann's face suddenly contorted and turned beet

red. She started making strange choking sounds while flapping her hands quickly up and down.

"What's gotten into—" And then Jennifer realized it, too. "Where the heck is Teri? Weren't the two of you car pooling?"

"I thought Suzy was going to strangle me, and I made a run for it. Fortunately, I had driven my car, but I forgot all about—"

A knock sounded on the door, making all three women jump and Muffy woof. This was just great! All they needed was one more act for this circus. No telling what her neighbors thought was going on.

Through the peephole, Jennifer could see Teri's anxious face, and a man dressed all in white standing so close to the door, she couldn't identify him. She opened the door.

"All we can hope for now is to find the body," Teri said as she swept past Jennifer. "We stayed right on their tail until Forsyth, and then it was like both cars evaporated off the face of the earth. We went by Leigh Ann's apartment, but we couldn't find her Nissan and no one was there. The door's locked. I thought you ought to know before someone comes—oh!" She paused, spotting Leigh Ann on the sofa and Suzy in the chair. "No blood?"

"Everything's fine," Jennifer said, nudging Teri farther into the room. Gus was still in the doorway, his head shaking slowly back and forth, his handsome face drawn. He raised his hands and said, *"Madre de Dios,"* and Jennifer pulled him into the room, closing the door.

"Why—" Jennifer began.

Teri pointed an accusatory finger at Leigh Ann. "She just *had* to tell one of the other waitresses that Roy had asked her to his family reunion, and, of course, Suzy overheard it, or so I was told."

Suzy cringed.

Gus flew to Leigh Ann, kissing the tips of her fingers and chattering so fast that Jennifer had no hope of following anything with her meager two years of high school Spanish.

"Roy had already gone for the day," Teri continued. "I figure that's why she went after Leigh Ann." She looked at Suzy, who flushed a bright red. "I'm not quite sure what happened after that, but I saw the two of them, first Leigh Ann and then Suzy, fly out of the kitchen, through the lobby, and into the parking lot."

Gus was now down on one knee, stroking Leigh Ann's hand. Jennifer did catch *"te quiero."*

She had always admired the way Spanish left no confusion about a man's intentions. Literally *te quiero* meant *I want you.* A girl knew where she stood, not like in English where the word "love" could as easily be directed at a good book or a tasty slice of pie.

Jennifer made a double take. Gus had stopped chattering and was making his way up Leigh Ann's arm with little wet kisses. And now Leigh Ann was answering back— in Spanish. That girl was a whole box of tricks.

"I was balancing an Eddie and two beers," Teri continued, "so it wasn't like I could just drop it in the laps of the customers I was serving and go after them. But then, here comes Gus running out of the kitchen, hollering *'¡Muerte! ¡Muerte!'* I wasn't quite sure what that meant, but I knew it couldn't be good. So I excused myself— which means I lost my tip for the whole meal—I hope you plan to make it up to me, Leigh Ann—grabbed my purse and Gus, and we took off after them in his truck. When we couldn't find them, I thought I'd better let you know."

Teri collapsed onto the sofa next to Leigh Ann, who

seemed totally preoccupied with Gus. "If you're going to scare me like that, the least you could do is really be hurt."

Leigh Ann turned in Teri's direction. "I'll see what I can do next time."

"Could you please get him up?" Jennifer asked, motioning toward Gus.

Muffy let out a loud yawn and sauntered toward the bedroom. Apparently she'd had all she could handle for the evening, and so had Jennifer.

"Okay, everybody's fine. Let's call it an evening." Jennifer clapped her hands. "Everybody out."

"But señorita, *un momento por favor*," Gus said. "You want to know who knocked off old man Walker?"

Jennifer stared at Teri.

"It was a long car ride. We had to talk about something."

Jennifer looked back at Gus. "Yes."

"If I were you, I'd check out this Benny dude," Gus said without any hint of an accent.

"*Benny dude?* I thought you didn't speak much English."

"Sometimes people assume." Gus shrugged. "And it keeps Roy off my back."

"What do you know about Benny?"

"Just that he has the hots for Lisa. Hey, man, old man Walker was too old for a chick like her. Besides, I overheard Benny telling her not to worry, that he'd take care of her now and that the two of them could run the restaurants together. Make *mucho dinero*."

Jennifer felt stunned. She'd seen Lisa and Benny together with her own eyes but hadn't really suspected that Benny might have killed his uncle. But what better motive could someone have than money *and* love?

Chapter 25

How long did it take to find out everything there was to know about a person anyway?

Jennifer fidgeted in her seat at the Mexican restaurant two blocks down from her apartment. She'd had about all the free chips and salsa the waiter was going to give her, considering the line at the entrance waiting for supper, and Sam still hadn't shown.

She could write down the facts of her own life in one short paragraph. Born Macon, Georgia. Reared Baptist. College graduate. Current part-time caterer; full-time rejection accumulator. Ambitions: to be a published mystery novelist and someday a mother. Caretaker of former greyhound racing star. (The star part was not really true, but Muffy would always be a winner in her heart.) Two arrests, if the contempt of court charge counted. Key witness in one murder case and star witness in Atlanta's current and most notorious murder case. Major liability to anyone unfortunate enough to befriend her.

See? How hard could it be?

Sam promised he'd have something for her about Benny by tonight, and he knew not to promise if he couldn't deliver. She didn't like disappointments. Her mother had never told her when she was taking her to the latest Disney flick, just in case it was sold out. One tantrum on hard pavement in front of most of Macon's population of five-year-olds was apparently quite enough. And she'd made the same promise to Jaimie. Life already came with enough disappointments.

Again she caught the eye of her waiter. Oh, no. He was grinning back. He must think she was flirting with him. She'd have to throw him off by ordering some nachos. He was heading toward her when Sam appeared in the doorway. He spoke to the hostess and then joined her. The waiter, thank goodness, veered off.

" 'Bout time," she greeted him.

"My sentiments exactly. Did you order for us?"

"Actually I did, but I asked them not to give it to the kitchen until you arrived. You're forty-five minutes late."

"And well worth the wait." He grinned at her.

She hoped he was referring to what he'd found out and not his own charming presence. "Spill it!"

The waiter brought Sam water, took his drink order, and assured them their food would be out soon. Then he winked at Jennifer.

Sam unfolded his napkin and took a sip of water. He was toying with her. Not wise. Their eyes locked and he got the message.

"Okay. Benny was not the best kid on the block. His physical characteristics let him in for some heavy teasing, but he developed a reputation for not playing fair, which solved most of his problems."

She'd always thought calling a bare-handed, 110-pound kid pitted against a two-hundred-pound bully a fair fight somewhat ludicrous. He probably had learned early that *fair* in his case meant *lose.*

"I think he had an arrest, maybe two, but all those

records are sealed, of course. His mother Alma is indeed Emma's sister by blood, and their father was a school administrator who made a comfortable living, supplemented by Alma's family's money. The father died five years ago followed shortly by Alma, leaving the kids a tidy nest egg but not enough to call themselves rich.

"Babs is the oldest by nine minutes. Neither has ever been married. Both live in the same town-house development, one block away from each other. They were business majors at the University of Georgia, graduating the same year with grade point averages within two-tenths of a percentage of one another. Both drive BMWs. But Babs went through a red period during which she dyed her hair and sang with a rock band with whose drummer she shared more than a professional relationship."

"Would I have heard of this group?"

"No. Benny apparently keeps his rebellious side, if he has one, to himself. For a while he worked for a chain of computer stores. He seldom dates and definitely has had no serious relationships. When Edgar started his expansion, he offered each of them a restaurant to manage. Babs jumped at the chance. Gigs were getting further and further apart for the band, and the drummer had since taken up with a saxophonist."

"And Benny agreed, too," Jennifer added.

"After some coaxing from Babs and Emma. He had been offered a district manager's position by that time, but the chain he was with was getting battered by the competition. They've since gone under."

The waiter delivered Sam's beer and another burning stare at Jennifer. "How'd you find all this out?"

"Here and there. Their high school is having a reunion, and the committee is interviewing old friends and current acquaintances to put together some surprise nostalgia clips, kind of who you were, what you did, and where you are now."

"Really?" Jennifer asked. "And you got all that from the committee?"

He looked down his nose at her. "I *am* the committee."

She tried to cover fast. "I knew that."

The waiter brought their food, a sizzling steak fajita for Sam (her concession to his hard work) and chiles rellenos for her. Hers had an extra scoop of sweet corn pudding.

"So you think he killed Edgar to be with Lisa?" she asked.

Sam shook his head, finishing his bite of steak. "That was your idea, not mine. Nobody I talked to made mention of them as a couple. If they had something going on prior to Edgar's death, they must have kept it quiet."

"They had to have known each other for the past ten years, all the time Edgar and Lisa were married," Jennifer concluded. "If he'd fallen really hard for her, that might explain his lack of interest in other women."

Sam nodded, but she could tell he didn't think that was it. Some people could live a lifetime on one love letter. But others seemed to have a more practical, love-the-one-you're-with attitude. Apparently, Benny didn't strike Sam as the love-letter type.

"You may be right, but my impression is that Benny is more of a numbers man. You have to ask, if he was as successful as he appeared to be, why did he decide to join the family business?"

"Emma told me he was going to inherit it one day. He and Babs. At least Emma's fifty-one percent."

"Yeah? Well, add that to Lisa's forty-nine—"

"And he gets it all."

Chapter 26

"Stop gloating and keep digging," Jennifer ordered.

Teague McAfee dusted off his jeans and handed her a stack of back issues of the *Atlanta Eye*. The cramped, dark room of the tabloid's morgue had a faint smell of mold that tickled her nose. She fought off a sneeze.

Ever since Mrs. Walker had told her about Edgar's affair with another woman, she'd been dying to know who it was. If she were lucky, the affair might yield another suspect she could throw at Arlene Jacobs, at least until she could get the goods on Lisa. Or Benny.

She'd picked up the phone and dialed McAfee's number at least a dozen times, slamming it down before it rang. Finally, she'd swallowed all her pride and done it. McAfee, true to form, was worse than she even imagined he'd be.

"I knew you'd come to me, Marsh." He didn't even try to suppress his grin. He was beaming.

As irritating as it was, she'd had to accept it. She needed gossip, old gossip, and she couldn't figure out any other way to get it. Mrs. Walker was protecting someone or something. She'd lied, and although Jennifer felt the woman probably had good reason, she could no longer completely trust her friend to do what was best for her case.

"It might help if we had some idea what we were looking for," Teague complained.

"I told you. Any kind of scandal to do with Edgar Walker thirty or so years back. Why don't you have this stuff on microfiche, anyway?"

Her nose itched, but she didn't dare scratch it. Her hands were the powdery gray of smeared newsprint.

"Doesn't seem to be much call for research into the kinds of stories we write. People throw our news out with the next day's garbage."

How appropriate.

They'd made it through all of two year's worth of tasteless antics by various Atlantans and a few tales more appropriate to *The X-Files* than to a newspaper. But nothing about one Edgar Walker.

"You've got to remember, this guy didn't become newsworthy until his business took off a few years ago. Money, sex, weird stuff—that's what sells, but the public has to know who we're writing about, unless the weird stuff is weird enough."

Jennifer sat back and brushed the hair out of her eyes. "Well, then, maybe we're looking for the wrong flag. Mrs. Walker's family was prominent, right? Their name would have been known."

"She was an Albright?"

Jennifer nodded.

"You don't hear much about them anymore, not since the old man died. But I know the name, even at my age. Made and lost two fortunes. The last one he held on to, though."

"Okay, then. Look for his name."

She sniffed loudly—if it wasn't mold, it had to be dust—and dug into another stack. Close to the bottom she caught the name in a headline. She pulled out the copy, leaned back against the stacks, and scanned the front page. Inch-high letters announced that Emma's father was backing some big Hollywood film while romancing the leading lady on the side.

"Is this true?" she asked, offering it to Teague.

He took it and glanced over the newsprint. "Nah. The picture's spliced. We do it better these days."

She dropped the newspaper back where it belonged and sighed. Her back ached and her knees weren't doing so great either. Why had she thought she could find the truth here?

"Okay, I think I've got something." Teague pulled out another issue. On the cover was a full-length picture of a much younger Edgar Walker. Not bad. Maybe Jennifer had been a little hasty in dismissing him. Maybe Emma did have some taste in men after all—at least in their looks.

Next to Edgar's photo was another full-length picture of a striking woman wearing an evening gown and looking back over her shoulder, her long, light-colored hair flowing, her smile elegant. Inset in an oval between the two of them was a young, attractive Emma Walker.

Somehow Jennifer had never actually considered the idea that Emma might have ever looked any way other than she did now. It was a startling idea.

Her gaze wandered to the headline, which read: AL-BRIGHT SON-IN-LAW STEPS OUT.

"That one might be true," Teague told her.

"How do you know that?"

"They didn't doctor the photos. If you've got a story, why make one up?"

Why make one up at all? she wondered, but kept it to

herself. No reason to alienate Teague at this point. She might need him again. "Think I could have a copy of this?"

"It comes with a price."

She'd known when she called him that Teague McAfee gave nothing away. The question was simply how much it was going to cost her.

"And that is . . . ?"

"I want an exclusive. *Your* exclusive."

Terrific. Every writer needed publicity, but she really would prefer that it be in the legitimate press. And what would Sam say if he saw her face across the cover of the *Atlanta Eye*?

"Okay."

"Okay? Just like that? I don't have to cajole or beg? Just okay?"

"Just okay. But not until after the trial."

He started to protest.

"Take it or leave it."

She had a firm grip on the copy, and she'd wrestle him for it if she had to.

Teague studied her face. "Okay, Marsh, but I expect enough material to fill a whole page."

She'd give him material all right. The question was whether or not he'd want to print it.

Jennifer swept into the lobby of the *Macon Telegraph* like a woman on a mission and ran smack into Sam, who was on his way out. She caught her breath and demanded, "Where are you going?"

"And good afternoon to you, too." He winked at her, clearly amused. "I was coming to find you. What are *you* doing here?"

She offered him the copy of the thirty-year-old story from the *Atlanta Eye*. "You gotta see this."

He took it from her. "What are you doing with this trash?" he asked as he unrolled it.

So much for his good mood. One innocent mention of the tabloid press was enough to turn this seeker of truth into a major grump.

"It's a story about Edgar Walker," she offered, hoping to soothe his irritation. He was, after all, a sweetheart—most of the time.

"The *Eye* is the worst example of tabloid journalism you can find anywhere. You can't believe a word they print. I wouldn't wipe my shoes with it. I wouldn't subject my bird—"

"You don't have a bird." She nudged Sam. The receptionist was watching them intently.

Sam offered the woman a boyish grin—fake, but real enough looking. "If anyone comes looking for me, tell them I got a lead in the Walker case." Then he grabbed Jennifer by the elbow and shuffled her outside.

It had gotten too hot and was threatening rain, one of those quick afternoon showers that washed the heat out of the air and then cleared, leaving frizzy hair in its path.

They walked several blocks up the street and ducked into a coffee shop/bookstore. It was dark, the only natural light coming from the storefront windows, which were obscured with posters announcing poetry readings and promoting herbal remedies. They took a table in the far rear surrounded by shelves of books on three sides.

"Now what the heck—"

"Thirty years ago Edgar Walker had an affair," Jennifer began.

"Says who? The *Atlanta Eye*?"

She shook her head. "Emma mentioned it to me. Lisa wasn't his first. Besides, the pictures aren't spliced, which means, most likely, that the story is true. Teague said—"

Sam glared at her. "What the heck were you doing with McAfee?"

No reason to let him get off on his dislike of McAfee. She suspected Sam harbored the tiniest bit of jealousy where Teague was concerned, and she had no time to deal with that right now.

"What'd you promise him to get this?"

Her face went beet red. "Would you just keep with the program? The fact is, Edgar Walker had an affair."

Sam could have pushed it, but he didn't. "So what if Walker was sleeping around? Old dog, old trick. Who cared—other than Emma?"

"No, you don't understand. It happened while Emma's dad was alive. It was a big scandal. If you'll just take a minute to look at this . . ." She pulled the paper from his hand and laid it flat on the small table. "See? And they couldn't divorce. She told me so."

"Why not?" Sam asked. "How many times did he have to stray before Emma figured it out? She doesn't strike me as a slow study."

"No, don't you see? It was that pride thing—her pride. Emma had taken up with this guy against her father's wishes—at least initially. She insisted on marrying him. It was that 'I made my bed, now I've got to lie in it' routine."

"So? That happened to lots of women. What is it that I'm not following here?"

"It's not that Edgar had an affair, and it's not that Emma stood by him. Look at who he had the affair with."

She thumped her hand loudly at the caption under the picture.

Sam pulled it closer. "Thelma Ornsby?"

"Right. Ornsby as in Walter, as in the Walkers' attorney, as in I bet he didn't much care for Edgar."

Sam shook his head. "I don't know. That was a long time ago."

"It was his little sister, for Heaven's sake. And Edgar wasn't just messing with his sister, he was doing it on the front page of the *Atlanta Eye*. Do you think a brother ever gets over that, especially a proud son of the South?"

"Point taken. Okay, so what are you trying to tell me? Ornsby killed Edgar defending his sister's honor—thirty years late?"

Telling him? Did she have a point to all this? "Yes. Maybe. No. I don't know, but I think the last place I'd entrust my dollar was with some guy I'd—"

"What can I get you?" the waitress asked.

"A mocha cappuccino," Jennifer said immediately. She'd smelled it when they walked in.

"Black coffee," Sam added.

"And would you like that with—"

"No. Just hot, just black, just coffee."

Just go.

"Listen to me." Jennifer was sitting on her knees on the wooden chair, every nerve of her body alive.

"Settle," Sam ordered. "I'm hearing you. But I don't know what it means, and I don't want to have to pick you up off the floor."

And she didn't either. She sat down properly on the chair. Maxie would know. She thought she'd had this big revelation to share with Sam, but what was the use of finding a big, bright puzzle piece if she didn't have all the edge pieces fitted together?

"Why were you looking for me?" she asked.

"I got word back on those fingerprints off the glasses we took from Brewster's apartment."

At last, something tangible. "Yes, and . . . ?"

"And nothing. No matches in the police database."

Jennifer sighed and sat back.

"What? You thought Natalie Brewster was a felon? I told you I was pretty sure we wouldn't get anything from the prints."

"And the hair?"

"You were right. It was dyed. Actually, it was coated with one of those temporary rinses. Originally it had been a medium brown with reddish highlights."

The waitress plunked down their coffees. "What else can I get you? We have some unbelievable French pastries made fresh this morning."

The coffees were rent for the table. They hadn't come in to eat. Sam shooed her away.

Jennifer took a sip of her drink. It had been topped with whipped cream, and it was heavenly. Thick, rich, caloric. "Did you ever get the information about the bank records?" She swirled the thick cream on top with her finger.

"Yeah. Guess I forgot to tell you."

Forgot to tell her? She reminded herself to be nice. And made a mental note that some things she should do herself. She waited, but he sat sipping his coffee.

"*What* did you forget to tell me?"

"Oh, you mean the records. Everything's fine as best I could tell. No withdrawals on the franchise accounts, at least. No missing funds."

Jennifer sat back and let out a deep breath. Natalie Brewster wasn't a felon and she wasn't a thief. Yet she'd gone to great lengths to adopt a dead woman's identity. Why?

"This puts us back to square one," she said.

"Only with Brewster. I think you moved us forward a square with this Ornsby revelation."

Sam was trying to make her feel better. She could tell from the way he looked at her from under his eyelashes, like a little boy telling a fib. He could be sweet like that. But his words couldn't change the facts. What she'd found out about Ornsby moved them sideways, not forward. And the more they seemed to uncover, the less certain she was about what really happened to Edgar Walker.

Chapter 27

Bigsby had turned out to be a bigger player in this mystery than Maxie had suspected. Rufus Donaldson had had an affair with Bigsby's sister thirty-two years ago. And not a private affair, either. It had hit all of the papers. Still, he had remained the family lawyer because . . .

Because, because, because—think, Jennifer!

. . . because Emily Donaldson had insisted upon it.

That *had* to be why. Emma must have told Edgar she wanted Walter Ornsby to handle their affairs. She had most of the money. She had the power to keep him. And Edgar had a lot to atone for. But even if she were right, Jennifer couldn't think of a single reason why Ornsby would stay.

An even bigger question was the true identity of Natalia Brewski, the woman who had passed herself off as having a plan to sell Chocolate Heaven fudge in kiosks in every mall in America. She looked the part, she seemed to know what she was doing, and yet she wasn't who she said she was. No, she was . . .

"Okay, Maxie, give it up!" Jennifer demanded, wanting to shake her monitor until the words magically appeared. She had typed in everything Maxie could possibly need to know about the woman calling herself Natalie Brewster and the latest on Edgar's escapades. The least Maxie could do was come up with some answers. Too bad she didn't have a *solve* button on her computer like the old *total* key on calculators.

She shook her head. She needed a fresh perspective, a new eye. She'd take some of her writing to the critique group that night. Maybe one of the gals would see the logic in the mess.

April's hormones must have been raging. That was the only way Jennifer could explain the array of finger foods that took up most of Monique's Queen Anne dining room table. She wasn't particularly hungry herself, which was probably fortunate since April was devouring everything within reach. Apparently she was eating not only for two but for all future generations of little Aprils.

April chomped down on another chicken wing, wiped her hands on a napkin and demanded the page Jennifer had just finished reading. Normally, they didn't pass around printed pages, preferring to get the impact of the spoken word. But something she had read must have bothered April. Jennifer tossed the paper across the table.

April pursed her lips as she tapped her greasy index finger lightly against the page. "You know how much I like Maxie Malone . . . and your style, as always, is really good, but . . ." she began, licking the fingers of her other hand.

Jennifer leaned forward, almost catching her hair in the pecan squares before tucking it behind her ears. April was using the *b* word: *but*. The word was never good. It automatically negated anything positive that came before it. Kind words and then the ax. It was sort of like offering someone a pillow before chopping off her head.

"The plot is . . . not exactly . . ." April scrunched her

eyes together and then opened them wide. "Did you try some of this dip?" She pushed the bowl toward Jennifer.

"I think what April is trying to say . . ." Leigh Ann started as she reached past Jennifer and dunked a corn chip into the sour cream-black olive mixture. She brought the chip close to her lips and then, looking Jennifer full in the face, stopped. "I don't write mystery, so what do I know?"

Coward.

At least Leigh Ann was looking better than she had the last time she saw her. Now that she and Teri had quit their jobs at the restaurant and Suzy had replaced them as her undercover source, they had returned almost to their normal selves. They seemed able to stay awake during a critique meeting, which, at the moment, was not necessarily desirable.

Jennifer looked across the table at Teri, who was having none of the goodies and who, in lieu of her perpetual exercising, had pulled her legs into a lotus position in one of the dining chairs. Teri seemed lost in thought, studying her in a kind of sad, pitying way.

This was like getting terminal news from a doctor. Kind of an "I'm sorry to inform you your book has flat-lined."

Teri clenched her jaw and then spoke. "You're too good a friend to let this go."

Words of death. Jennifer didn't need friends *that* good.

"What these two yellow-bellies are afraid to tell you," Teri went on, "is that your plot stinks. Where did you come up with such an idiotic idea in the first place? You've got some woman masquerading as a kind of kiosk expert and running some kind of scam, but she doesn't make off with the dough. And then there's some dude's sister getting used and abused thirty years ago, not to mention strange nephews, and another somebody's cousin twice removed, or whatever the heck it was—"

"Teri." All Monique had to do was say her name. It stopped her cold. Teri slumped back in her chair like a scolded dog. She had crossed the bounds of good critique etiquette, and she knew it.

"Jennifer," Monique said kindly, shoving a bowl of peanuts in her direction as if they would somehow soften the blow she was about to throw.

She hated Monique's condescending kindness more than anything else—anything except Monique's supercilious teacher mode.

"While our books are unabashed fiction, we must all strive for a certain semblance of real life."

Sure. Monique set her fiction on a planet with two suns and had a hero who was a silicon-based thingoid who communicated by clicking his tongue. She was supposed to take advice about reality from her?

"It's obvious that in an attempt to make your work more real," Monique continued, "you've taken an element or two from Mrs. Walker's current situation to weave into Maxie's case. Where I think you've fallen down is in your selection of subplots. We don't understand how they fit, how they're all going to come together toward a coherent solution. Our role as authors is to bring order to the chaos of possible events in any particular situation. While interesting, your plot currently shows more chaos than order. Do you understand what I'm getting at?"

Monique was sounding a little too much like some of the rejection letters Jennifer had stacked in her closet. She'd much prefer for Monique to spit it out like Teri had. To just tell her that the book was a waste of good trees.

"In the past," Monique added, smiling down her nose,

and ladling out a cup of punch which she handed to Jennifer, "while your plots tended toward the fanciful, there was always a basis—however farfetched—that the reader could relate to, find some kind of pattern—"

Jennifer shook her head. "You're all missing the point. Real life is complicated. Didn't you get it when Maxie—"

"Uh-uh," Teri interrupted. "Flew right over this head."

Leigh Ann nodded and sucked down an olive.

"You know better, Jennifer." Now Monique was shaking *her* head. "We don't defend our work. It's either on the page or it isn't. A book doesn't come with a copy of the author attached to explain what the reader doesn't understand."

Jennifer had used that argument just last week about a scene Monique had read. How she hated it when someone turned her own words against her. She should never have uttered a word about that chapter. It was payback time.

And Monique wasn't finished. "I'm assuming you've outlined the rest of the book and know exactly where you're going with this. Would you like to fill us in on how you plan to end it? Maybe then we could see if all the elements you've included are going to work for you."

Teri, Leigh Ann, and April all turned toward her.

Monique knew she didn't outline, that she wrote by the seat of her pants. Besides, how could she? She didn't have a clue what was going to happen next. But if Maxie didn't do something soon, Emily Donaldson was headed straight for prison.

Jennifer set the punch, untouched, on the table. She was angry even though she knew she shouldn't be. Take it or leave it. They spoke the truth. The story wasn't making any sense—not to her, not to them, not to Maxie.

They all looked so concerned, so caring, so sure she'd

lost what little talent she had ever possessed. So certain that her plot was too big a jumble to be believable, too big a confused mess to ever make any sense. And suddenly she saw it, too. They were right.

She'd been going about this solution business all wrong. What she needed was a fresh approach. She had to answer each question separately, one at a time, and worry about how the whole thing fit together later. No more compound questions. She needed to know who Natalie Brewster was before she could even think about what role she played in this mess. She needed to know who had a big enough grudge against Edgar Walker that they would actually kill him.

But first she needed to know what Emma Walker was really doing at Edgar Walker's estate the night he was killed.

Chapter 28

"How lovely of you to surprise me with a visit, Jennifer," Mrs. Walker said, hugging her with surprising ferocity. "I was just thinking about you."

When the older woman let go, Jennifer thought she detected a tear in her eye. It was the first time she'd ever seen her cry, and it almost broke Jennifer's heart.

"You know my trial begins tomorrow," Mrs. Walker continued, composing herself, "and I'm feeling a bit alone."

Anyone with Tiger for a pet could never feel entirely alone, Jennifer reminded herself, as she felt a tug on her shoe. The dog was untying the laces of her sneakers and tangling them around himself as he growled and spit as though trying to pull a worm from the ground.

Mrs. Walker bent down and extracted the creature, excused herself, and carried him down the hall. She returned a moment later without him and carrying a china coffee cup and saucer.

"I hope you don't mind, dear, but I don't want Tiger to hear what it is I'm about to say."

Jennifer didn't mind at all, but she didn't like the ominous tone in Mrs. Walker's voice, and she wasn't at all sure she was going to like what she was about to hear.

"Shall we? I was just about to have some morning refreshments," Mrs. Walker explained, leading Jennifer into the living room, where a full silver service of coffee was waiting on the coffee table. She set the cup and saucer down next to her own.

The two women fell silent as they sat on the couch. Jennifer watched Mrs. Walker's gaze wander out the window. She had no doubt that her thoughts had nothing to do with the morning energy of the city.

Jennifer squeezed the older woman's hand. It was deathly cold, and the lump in Jennifer's throat grew even bigger. "We've got to believe everything will be all right, that the truth will come out," Jennifer said.

She had come to Mrs. Walker's condo to confront her, to force the truth from her, but Emma looked so fragile, so alone, so vulnerable that Jennifer was having trouble finding the words. She was an old lady with no husband, no children, and an improbable beast for a pet. If she were found guilty, who would visit her in prison? Her friends were people very like herself. And Mae Belle and Jessie didn't even drive.

"Tiger is rather an acquired taste, I'm afraid," Mrs. Walker began, continuing to stare at the city outside, "but he is so terribly fond of you."

If that was fondness, she'd hate to see what he did to someone he *didn't* like.

"If I'm no longer able to care for him," Mrs. Walker turned her large, blue eyes on Jennifer, "I want you to promise you'll take him."

God was punishing her. She'd made an error in judgment by getting up in the middle of the night to go out to Edgar's estate (where she had no business whatsoever) and setting off the pool alarm before Mrs. Walker could wake up and escape. And now she was going to have to pay for it by taking in Tiger. Poor Muffy. Poor Jennifer.

"You will take him, won't you?"

Jennifer fought back tears, and the worst part was she wasn't sure if she was crying for Mrs. Walker or herself. "Of course," she croaked. And she meant it. Tiger would die—of old age—in her arms. If it came to that.

Mrs. Walker let out a huge sigh and smiled. "Thank goodness. I'm so relieved! I have no idea what I would have done if you'd said no."

Jennifer cleared her throat. "Have you decided about the plea arrangement they offered you?"

"Oh, I couldn't accept something that was a lie, dear." The energy had returned to Mrs. Walker's voice. "I couldn't live with myself in or out of prison. When it comes right down to it, our most important possession is honor, now isn't it? I can't say I killed Edgar when I didn't. It would defame his memory and allow his true murderer to go free. Coffee?"

Jennifer shook her head, the tears again welling in her eyes. It reminded her of the women accused at the Salem witch trials. Spare their lives by confessing the practice of Satanism or save their immortal souls and be hanged. She brushed the tears away with her fingertips.

"Oh, now, dear, you mustn't be upset. Everything will work out one way or another. It always does. Everyone is doing their very best—"

"No, they're not!" Jennifer exploded.

Mrs. Walker shrank back.

She hadn't meant to frighten the old dear, but anger was a lot easier to deal with than grief. And if she'd thought she had everything invested in this trial before, Tiger had upped the ante even more.

She lowered her voice. "I'm sorry, but your lawyers think you're guilty and your friends are being forced to testify against you."

Only one friend actually—Jennifer—but she felt better including herself in the company of others even if they were imaginary. "If all of us were doing everything we could, somebody would have found something, anything, to prove your innocence."

"My goodness. Now you've got yourself into a fret. You mustn't—"

"And you're the worst of all." There. She'd said it. She couldn't hold it in one second longer, and she knew if she didn't take the courage to say it before the trial started, she never would. "You've got to tell me why you were at Edgar's estate that night."

Mrs. Walker looked stunned. Calmly, she set down her coffee cup. "I don't know what to say."

"The truth." Jennifer whispered the words.

For several seconds Mrs. Walker studied her face. "I've caused you a lot of pain, haven't I? I'm so sorry. Edgar and I both made a lot of mistakes in our lives. People have been hurt. I didn't want to hurt anyone else."

That, Jennifer believed.

"Edgar began calling me about a year ago. He was very persistent. He wanted a reconciliation, said he'd been quite the fool in years past. At least he and I saw eye-to-eye on that one. He said he wanted us to grow old together. I pointed out to him that he was a bit late for that. We each seemed to have accomplished that feat quite nicely on our own. In any case, I blew him off, as you kids say. About six months ago he called again."

She looked at Jennifer. "I know you're going to think me quite foolish, but Edgar offered me something he knew

I could never resist—the plan for the franchise. All my life I've adored a challenge, and while I could never get interested in his restaurant business, the idea of dotting the country with something over which I'd had some small influence was thrilling."

"And that business about playing pranks on his estate?"

"There were never any pranks, dear. I got that off of TV. I could hardly tell Mae Belle and Jessie that Edgar and I were trysting."

"So you were meeting him to . . . ?"

"To discuss the plans for the franchise. He had this marvelous young woman helping him. She had some wonderful ideas, but he was never really confident in his own business ability."

"But why meet covertly, in the middle of the night? You had more right to make those decisions than Edgar did."

"I didn't want to hurt Edgar's relationship with Lisa. It was already under a strain, and she had worked so hard in the restaurant herself. How could I have condemned her as a home wrecker if I allowed any of my actions—however innocent—to wreck hers?

"The problem was that Edgar didn't trust Lisa's taste or her business acumen. It's not that she's stupid, dear, just unpolished."

And maybe Mrs. Walker simply needed to feel needed. "So you met with him."

She nodded. "At the pool house. I would come about midnight. Lisa goes to bed fairly early, you see, ten-thirty or eleven. Edgar always did suffer from a bit of insomnia, and I'm up all hours of the night. He would keep the dogs up. Turn off the alarms. Normally I'd come in through the fence. Two of the rails—"

"I know. I found them the night of the murder."

"Yes, well, I suppose you think it's terribly undignified of me, slipping through a fence and tromping about in the dark like that." There was a bit of a gleam in Mrs. Walker's eye. She might have aged on the outside, but she was still a bright-eyed sixteen-year-old inside, one who had been relegated to a world of bridge games and bingo. A night out in the dark must have seemed like an irresistible invitation to adventure.

"Normally Edgar met me, but he wasn't there that night. I assumed he'd been delayed somehow, so I made my way up to the cottage."

"Did you see anything in the pool?" Jennifer asked.

"Oh, you mean the body. Actually, I came around from the far side. I didn't want to get too close to the back of the house in case Lisa was still awake. I had noticed some lights when I came past the front, more than the normal security bulbs, that is."

"I don't suppose you saw anyone inside." Knowing Mrs. Walker as she did, she couldn't imagine her going past without a peek.

"Heavens no, dear. I'm too short to get much of a view, and I couldn't find a thing to stand on."

"And what did you find at the pool house?"

"Nothing. I was coming up the steps when I felt a tap on my shoulder, and I don't remember anything after that. Not until the alarm went off and you called to me."

"Why didn't you tell all of this to the police?"

"I did. All except the reason I was on the property. It didn't matter *why*, you see, only that I was there. You, Jessie, and Mae Belle would all have to testify to my going out to play pranks, as you put it. I didn't think it beneficial to have the police brand me a liar from the start. Besides, what possible difference could it make?"

Probably not much, with the kind of evidence lined up against Mrs. Walker.

The trial began tomorrow. It looked as if Mrs. Walker was doomed. Somehow, some way, Jennifer told herself, she had to find a way out. She had to keep from telling the prosecution what she'd seen that night at Edgar's estate.

Chapter 29

But Jennifer *had* been forced to testify. Arlene Jacobs had her declared a hostile witness and then ripped the truth from her.

She'd expected no less than a miracle. For Paul Drake to come dramatically through the courtroom doors and hand the attorneys a note, something, anything to exonerate Mrs. Walker. But it hadn't happened. And now, God help her, if her friend was convicted on her testimony, she'd carry the guilt with her to her grave.

She strained against the back of the passenger seat of Sam's car and brought her thoughts back to the here and now. They were somewhere on I-75 headed south, away from Atlanta and the scene of her betrayal.

"Are you going to stare out that window the rest of your life?" Sam asked.

She kind of liked that idea, considering how her life was going. At least he didn't sound quite so angry with her anymore.

"Look, I'm sorry I ragged on you," he said, reaching over and finding her hand. "It's not the two hundred dollars I had to put up for the contempt of court charge. It's not even the fact that I had to go to three ATMs—"

"I know," Jennifer said, more to herself than to him.

"I'm sorry, too." She rubbed the back of his hand with her thumb. He was every bit as worried about Mrs. Walker as she was.

"Something *will* break," he promised.

She didn't believe him any more than he believed himself. Yet it was good to hear the words, to send positive thoughts into the universe.

Who was she kidding? Mrs. Walker was going to fry.

She punched the car door. "I feel like breaking something."

"Do you think you could hold that thought until I can get you home and out of my car?"

She nodded, but she hardly heard his words. Something else was bothering her. Something had stuck in her mind when she'd thought back over everything that had happened, something that should have seemed obvious but somehow wasn't.

"I'd like to take you out tonight. Buy you dinner someplace nice," Sam offered.

He was being good. Real good. "Will there be dancing?" She liked dancing.

"Not by me, but I'm more than willing to watch."

She allowed herself a pout. Why was it most of the good ones couldn't dance? She never thought when she danced, and she could definitely do with a little less thinking. Too many unrelated ideas were cramming her brain.

"Of course, I'll have to go by the newspaper and file my story first."

Jennifer let out a loud groan.

"What? It won't be that bad, I promise. I won't quote you."

No, he wouldn't, but he wasn't the only reporter in court. "I was thinking about Teague McAfee's story."

Sam actually cringed. It was going to be even worse than she'd imagined, and there wasn't a single thing she could do about it.

"Do you think he has a journalism degree?" she asked.

"Don't remember."

"What do you mean you don't remember?"

"Just that, but I'm sure I could find out. He applied for a job with the *Telegraph* a couple of years ago. If he'd been hired, I would have been the one to train him. If you're really that curious, when I get to the office I'll see if I can find it in my files. And if I don't have it, I'm sure personnel—"

Jennifer bolted upright. "Turn the car around," she ordered, her hands fluttering up and down like a caged pigeon. What had been nagging at the back of her mind had finally coalesced. They had to get back to Atlanta.

Sam let go of her hand and grasped the wheel. "What?"

"You heard me. Turn around."

"We're on a major highway. We can't just turn around."

"Okay, then take the next exit."

"Where're we going?"

"Emory University. She could be at the alumni office. If we don't find her there, we'll check the registrar's. It almost has to be one or the other."

"Who's the she?"

"The woman calling herself Natalie Brewster—how did she know that Brewster was dead?" Jennifer turned in her seat and hovered close to Sam. She could feel the adrenaline rushing through her veins.

He gave her a skeptical sideways glance and shrugged. "Obituaries? Old newspaper reports?"

"If so, how did she get Brewster's transcripts sent to the Down Home Grill?"

"I imagine she wrote a formal request, forged a signature and sent in a money order—"

Jennifer shook her head. "No way. You said yourself the records were clearly marked. The woman was dead. Nobody would have sent out those reports unless . . ."

"Unless what?"

"Didn't you tell me you had trouble getting access to the alumni records?" Jennifer could barely sit still as this section of the puzzle started falling into place.

"Do you think you could finish one coherent thought before starting another?" Sam asked.

"Just answer the question. Did you have trouble getting a look at the alumni information?"

"Not really. The woman who was supposed to help me was busy someplace else. I had to wait until someone was free."

"Just stepped out, as in when you stepped in?" Jennifer added.

"Something like that."

"As in she saw you, recognized you, and ran for cover."

"What?"

"Don't you see? It explains how she knew the name of a dead MBA graduate and how she had access to her files and how she could get a transcript sent, because she sent it herself."

"Are you expecting me to follow any of this?"

Jennifer stared at him. Sometimes Sam could be so dense. "Our Natalie Brewster impersonator—she has to work at Emory."

"Stay!" Jennifer ordered Sam in the hallway outside the alumni office. "If she sees you, she'll bolt. She's going to be scared enough anyway, and the fact that you're a reporter—"

"This is nuts. Do you know that?"

A woman passing by with an armful of folders looked at them strangely.

Jennifer shushed him. "We've got a real chance at finding out who this woman is, and—"

Sam took her by the shoulders. "Jennifer," he said with deep, baritone authority.

Sometimes he sounded just like her father had, and while she loved them both—well, loved her father and maybe, someday, could love Sam—she didn't need him pulling some kind of paternal power play on her.

She leaned in close and whispered, "Trust me. If I'm wrong, I'm wrong, and I'll pay for dinner."

"This from a woman who couldn't make her court payment?"

"Next week. I'll take you out next week."

"Look. I don't want you getting your hopes up over some leap of logic."

Leap of logic? It was the easiest, most logical solution, considering the facts at hand. An employee would know about a deceased graduate and have the ability to send out a transcript without arousing suspicion. She had to be right. But she'd never find out standing in the hallway.

"Let me go in with you," Sam insisted.

"I can scream really loud, and I will if I need you. Now, stay here." She pecked him on the cheek. "Be back in a sec."

Then she took a deep breath and pulled open the glass door to the office.

Three desks were visible. The one on the left was occu-pied by a pleasant, middle-aged woman with short, white hair. At the one on the right sat an attractive African-American woman.

And right in the middle, her desk pulled forward enough to make it evident that she was the receptionist, sat an unassuming, slimly built young woman with shoulder length, reddish brown hair. She looked up with large gray eyes as Jennifer approached.

No femme fatale here. But then the girl smiled, a beautiful, engaging smile. Add some more mascara to those long lashes, eyeliner, a little shadow to highlight those enormous lids, a darker shade of lipstick, blush, green contact lenses, hair dye, a wonder bra. Okay, so she was talking major make-over, but it almost seemed possible.

"May I help you?" she asked with what appeared to be genuine curiosity. That was a gift. Making it seem as if she'd never asked that question before, as if she was actually interested in what had brought Jennifer Marsh to Emory's alumni office that afternoon.

Jennifer cleared her throat. "I'm trying to locate an old high school chum." *Good going, Jen. Wow the girl with your hip lingo.*

"Well, let's see what I can do to help you." She turned to her computer keyboard. "Name?"

"Brewster. Natalie."

The girl's fingers froze above the keys. She turned back and stared into Jennifer's eyes, the smile deserting her pale features.

Good. They understood one another.

"Maybe you'd like to get some coffee? Got a minute?" Jennifer asked.

The woman glanced over her shoulder to one of the women behind her. "I've got something I've got to take care of. I'll be back as soon as I can."

The woman didn't wait for a reply. She took her purse out of the drawer and stood up. She was close to Jennifer's height, just as Sam had said. Then she brushed past and, almost before Jennifer realized what was happening, was out the door.

Jennifer took off after her, only to run smack into Sam, who was standing with an arm around "Natalie" as if they were old friends, only this old friend had a good grip on the woman's upper arm.

Sam was smiling, but his words were less than friendly. "I'll be more than happy to call the police if that's what you want."

The woman shook her head. She looked dazed and confused, not at all the confident con artist that Jennifer had expected.

"Ready for that coffee?" Jennifer asked.

Chapter 30

"It's not that I wanted to steal someone's identity," the woman explained between sips of strong, black coffee. "It's more that I didn't want to be, couldn't be me, you know? Besides, Natalie wasn't using her name anymore, and it seemed a pity for her degree to go to waste."

She threw Jennifer a look as if what she was saying should somehow make sense.

"What's wrong with being you?" Sam asked from across the booth of the diner where he sat next to Jennifer.

The woman shrugged and stared into her coffee. "Nothing." She sat up straighter, and Jennifer guessed she'd been asking herself the same question for a long time.

It was a good question. This gal might be less striking than her version of Natalie Brewster, but she had an awful lot going for her—looks, personality, and vulnerability. Jennifer was having a hard time not liking her.

She had fully intended to despise "Natalie Brewster" once she'd found her. Somewhere in the deep, dark recesses of her soul, she'd even hoped "Natalie" was Edgar's murderer. Of course, if she were honest, she'd have to admit her motives had something more to do with Sam's reaction to "Natalie" than they did with her possible guilt. Honesty, at least to oneself, was sometimes overrated.

"Look, I know who he is," the woman said, motioning toward Sam, "but who are you, some undercover cop, a P.I., or what?"

That anyone would even consider for a moment that she could be a cop or a private eye was a stretch, but she kind of liked it. Maybe she had more presence than she thought.

It was her turn to sit up a little straighter. "I'm a friend of Emma Walker."

The woman allowed a half smile. "Yeah, Emma's all right."

"She didn't kill Edgar Walker," Jennifer assured her.

"I never thought she did. Is that why you're asking me all these questions? You want to pin Edgar's murder on me?"

"All we want are some answers to a few questions. You want to start with your name?" Jennifer asked. "We can easily find out on our own."

The woman took another long drink of coffee. She looked at them through half-lidded eyes and then spoke. "I suppose you could at that. I'm Allison Ornsby."

"Ornsby?" Sam repeated. Jennifer kicked him under the table. Better not to seem too surprised.

"Thelma's daughter and Walter Ornsby's niece," Jennifer stated as if she already knew it as fact.

The woman nodded.

"Edgar Walker was your father," she added, praying she wasn't about to make a major fool of herself.

The woman cocked her head at Jennifer and then nodded.

All of a sudden, Walter Ornsby's interest in Edgar's affairs made sense. Edgar must have kept him on to see that

Thelma and Allison were taken care of. That, or Walter had insisted—

"I don't want to talk to the press." The woman motioned toward Sam, who was gaping at her while he rubbed the ankle Jennifer had caught, a little harder than she'd intended, with her heel.

"Just ignore him," Jennifer assured her. "He prints anything we say here, and I'll personally break both his legs."

"One down, one to go," Sam said with a sideways glance at Jennifer.

Then suddenly he seemed all business, his professional demeanor back in place, the pain in his ankle, if indeed there was pain, apparently forgotten. "Why did you do it?" he asked, leaning forward.

"I don't know what it is you think I did."

"We're not accusing you of anything," Jennifer assured her. "Sam already checked the bank records. We know you didn't take any funds."

"You thought I—" Allison had a half-amused, half-disbelieving look on her face. "Oh, God, you're serious."

"Of course not," Jennifer covered fast, as if people swiped identities for the most innocuous of reasons.

Tears gathered in the corners of Allison's eyes. "Edgar didn't know who I was. I didn't get a chance to tell him before—" Her voice choked. "Mom died two years ago. I thought it was time I got to know my father."

"Why didn't you just—" Jennifer began.

"He knew where I was. He could have come to me anytime," she snapped.

Careless. Wasn't that how Emma had described Edgar? "Did Emma know about you?" Jennifer asked.

Allison shook her head. "At least I don't think so."

"Lisa?" Sam asked.

Again she shook her head.

"You weren't mentioned in Edgar's will," Jennifer said.

"Uncle Walter had set up a generous trust fund for me when I was born. My father paid into it. That was to be my inheritance. I guess he didn't want to leave any surprises when he was gone."

"But why take on the Natalie Brewster identity?" Sam asked.

"She had the credentials I needed. Uncle Walter mentioned something in passing about how successful the restaurants had become. New ones had been built all over the area, so I started studying the Grill. Business was really good, and I thought, why not take it national?"

"Then the idea for the franchise came from you?" Jennifer asked.

"Sure. I approached Edgar with it. The Down Home Grill is a sure bet. I've been taking courses for my MBA at night so I ought to know. But it's going to take a good while before I finish, with my working full-time."

"So you opted for an instant degree," Jennifer said.

"Only to work with my father. I'd already been working on a thesis about franchising, and I studied like crazy, so I'd know what I was talking about."

"I can testify to that," Sam agreed.

"I could have made it work, too," Allison added.

"And then?" Jennifer asked.

"And then I'd tell him who I was."

Ah, the fairy tale. She would prove herself worthy of her father's love and admiration, cast off her cloak of deceit, and he would embrace her into his loving family. There was a reason fairy tales were classed as fantasy.

"You got your Uncle Walter to make the introductions," Jennifer added.

Allison nodded. "At first he thought it was a really bad idea, but he couldn't say no to me. He never could."

"Did you see him a lot while you were growing up?" Sam asked.

"Mom had been married and divorced before she met my father. She wasn't young when I was born, almost forty. She never married again. Uncle Walter kind of watched over us."

"But how could your birth get past Emma? The affair between your mom and dad was on the cover of the *Atlanta Eye*."

Allison looked startled. "It was?"

Oops. Major faux pas. They were there to get information, not give it.

"Thirty years ago, hardly a paragraph." Jennifer didn't add that the pictures that went with that paragraph were six inches high.

"I was born in Marietta, and I grew up there," Allison explained. "I didn't move to Atlanta until after Mom died."

"What about that elaborate ruse with the apartment?" Sam asked.

"I had to have an address and a place to work out of in Brewster's name. I raided some of my trust fund, although, as it turned out, I really didn't need to. Edgar was paying me a really good salary. But I kept my regular job, taking off time here and there when I needed to. I let my classes go for a while and did most of my work on the franchise at night. Look, I'm telling you all this stuff, and I don't even know why you're asking."

The woman was right, assuming what she was saying was the truth. "We're trying to find out who killed Edgar."

Allison stared at her coffee.

"Don't you care?" Jennifer felt a tug on her sleeve. She shouldn't have said it, but she couldn't take it back now. The best she could do was apologize. "I'm sorry."

The young woman looked up. "No, you're right. I don't really care. The way I look at it, it must have been something he did that caused it. He was good at that."

"What?"

"Letting people down."

She stood up and walked out.

"What do you make of that?" Sam asked.

Jennifer shook her head. "It's hard for me to believe someone that cynical could still believe in fairy tales."

Chapter 31

Some people, like Allison Ornsby, made it through life without any family to speak of, and others seemed to have more than they could use.

Jennifer tapped the invitation against her cheek and then looked at it for the third time. It had come in the morning's mail.

You are cordially invited to the Mayfield Family Reunion to be held this Saturday at Lake Lorraine. Follow the signs. A covered dish lunch will be served at 1:00 P.M. Bring your favorites, your bathing suit, and don't forget your lawn chairs. Boat rides and skiing will be available, weather permitting.

At the bottom was scribbled a handwritten note.

Thought you might like to attend just in case you are kin. Maybe you can find someone who knows more about your great-grandmother. Look forward to seeing you. Melissa Bordeaux.

How sweet. And how convenient. Maybe things were looking up after all. If she could manage to stay out of

Lisa's way, she just might learn something. Somebody somewhere had to know about Lisa's intentions to kill Edgar. Who better to confide in than a member of the family?

She poured herself another cup of coffee and filled Muffy's bowl with water. Muffy looked at it and stuck her nose in the air. She obviously expected more from Jennifer, but she wasn't going to get it right now. Jennifer didn't have time.

Back at the keyboard, Maxie was plunging forward with her case.

"Miss Marsh, it's Suzy." Her voice over the phone was so muffled Jennifer could barely make out what she was saying. "I came in early because Louise is out again, and I got a chance to slip in the office when nobody much was around, and I think maybe I found something."

"Breathe," Jennifer reminded her.

A noisy rasp came over the line.

"Sorry. I get excited like that sometimes."

"Now what is it you think you've found?"

"I've always been really good at math, so I don't think it's me," she whispered.

"What's not you?"

"The books. Something's not quite right. It looks like ten percent is missing off the gross receipts."

"Are you sure?"

"Yeah."

"How far back?"

"As far back as I could check, at least a couple years."

"Someone was skimming?"

"No, I don't think so. It's not like it was stolen. It's

plainly marked, it's just I can't figure out who—oh, man! I've got to go. I think Lisa's—"

The phone went dead.

"Suzy?" Jennifer asked the dial tone.

Ten percent of the gross receipts was going where? Edgar was generous enough with his salaries, and Emma was raking in her share. Lisa benefited from Edgar's cut, both now and before. Roy was certainly well taken care of, even if he did hold the key to the restaurant's success. So who was getting the other ten percent?

Maybe Suzy was mistaken. She could have gotten things mixed up.

Jennifer dropped the receiver in its cradle and turned off the computer. She had something else she had to do right then—buy the ingredients for a dish to take to tomorrow's family reunion.

She never should have opened the door when Sam came knocking late last night, but she had. A knock on the door was like a ringing phone. She had to answer it. Sam just might have unearthed the crucial piece of information that would break Edgar's murder investigation wide open.

Not hardly. He'd only been checking on her.

When he saw the two gallons of potato salad she was making, he knew something was up, and it wasn't a luncheon she was catering with Dee Dee. And so here he was, in her car, her so-called date for somebody else's family reunion. She wondered if Suzy would say that made Sam and her pre-engaged.

She wound her Beetle over the dirt road that twisted down through thick foliage toward the lake. What had she been thinking? She had to be out of her mind to show up at Lisa's family reunion. Then again, it was almost worth it to see Sam in those shorts of his. He had cute knees. And he hadn't been much trouble, at least so far. He'd been napping for fifteen of the twenty-five minutes it took them to drive out to the lake. He never seemed to get any sleep— except when he was with her.

The cardboard signs printed with Magic Marker and staked at each turn made it clear she was heading in the right direction, but something in her gut told her there was trouble ahead. If this had been a horror movie, the black marker would have dripped into blood, warning, TURN BACK.

Sam stirred. "We there yet?"

"Time to get your shoes on."

"What? My shoes are on."

"Trip talk from when I was a kid. It means we're almost there."

The next curve brought them within sight of the water and a mass of cars nestled in a small clearing. She spotted Roy's Bronco. He and Suzy must be here. And then she saw Lisa's Jag. A little farther down the way was a car the same make and model as Leigh Ann's. For a moment it made her heart jump. Then she laughed. No way would Leigh Ann show up here.

Jennifer pulled forward and then backed up next to a sedan that was parked alongside the road. There wasn't really enough space, but she wedged in her Beetle so most of it was out of the road. It was well positioned should she need a quick getaway. She wasn't about to take the chance of someone blocking her in.

Sam yawned loudly and rubbed his face. His dark hair was mussed, and he looked cuter than he had any right to look. Once any unattached Mayfield women realized he wasn't family, he'd be like prime rib at a Kroger super sale. At least they would keep him occupied while she tried to get the information she needed.

It was a really hot day, and the bathing suit she had on under her shift was already sticking to her. Not that she would get in the water, even if she'd been there to enjoy the lake. She couldn't swim. Swimming took a leap of faith she'd never quite been able to accomplish.

She tossed him a tube of sunscreen. "Lather up."

"I don't intend—"

"And I don't intend to spend the evening slathering you with aloe."

"Is that what you'll do if I don't—"

"Put it on," she ordered with as much finality as she could muster. She stared at him until he opened the tube. Then she pulled a huge pair of black sunglasses from the glove compartment and shoved them on her face.

"Going incognito?" he asked.

She squirmed. "The sun bothers my eyes."

"Right."

Actually, she hoped that if she could avoid Lisa's seeing her head-on, she might get through most of the reunion unnoticed. Although Lisa did seem to have some kind of uncanny radar where she was concerned.

She popped the trunk, and Sam went around to the front of the car and retrieved two big Tupperware containers.

"So what's our cover?" he asked, shutting the trunk lid with his elbow. "What am I to you?"

In the interest of self-preservation, he obviously wanted to get their relationship straight before he suffered the consequences of another impromptu story. Smart fellow.

She draped her arms about his neck and leaned in between the containers. She whispered, "We're officially pre-engaged and I've—"

"Pre-engaged? That seems so tenuous."

"You have trouble with commitment. Anyway, I've brought you to meet the family I never knew I had. Great-Grandmama Mayfield disappeared off the face of the earth with no forwarding address."

"Abducted by aliens?"

"Quite possibly, but it might be better not to get into that."

They headed toward the picnic pavilion a few yards from the lake. People were everywhere. Most with dark hair, some faded to gray and others on to white. No taffy brown anywhere in sight, just as Melissa had said, although she did spy one redhead. Must be an in-law. And no bleach jobs. But Lisa had to be around somewhere.

Jennifer wedged the potato salad between a pasta dish and a huge bowl of chopped fresh fruit and then moved back onto the grass.

"Miss Marsh," a throaty voice called behind her. She turned and saw Melissa hobbling slowly toward her, a canvas medical shoe on one foot, her cane in hand. "So glad you could make it," she drawled. "And who's your young man? I don't think I've had the pleasure. . . ."

"Sam Culpepper." He offered his hand.

"Well, Mr. Culpepper, we're so glad you could join us. Please make yourself at home and enjoy. Gary is taking people around the lake on the pontoon. He should be back any minute. I think a few of them had the motorboat out skiing. Oh, there they go now."

She pointed her cane in the direction of the lake, where a teenage girl, one hand raised in a wave, whizzed by, pulled by a boat filled with wet passengers. "They're taking turns. I'm sure they'd be glad—"

"Maybe later," Sam assured her.

"Suit yourself. There's fishing, too, of course, although with all that noise and the way that boat's churning up the water, I doubt the fish are biting. Be sure to find yourself something to do while Miss Marsh visits. We'll be eating before long."

Jennifer watched as Melissa painfully made her way back down to a grouping of lawn chairs filled with the oldest generation of Mayfields.

"She seems like a nice lady."

"Oh, she is, but the poor dear is almost crippled with arthritis."

"Not to mention a bum foot."

"That, too."

Jennifer felt a poke in her back, and then Leigh Ann leaned around her shoulder, munching on a celery stick. "Hi, guys," she grinned. "Whoa, Sam. Where have you been hiding those knees?"

Jennifer almost lost it. "What the heck do you think you're doing here?" The place was already crowded without adding Leigh Ann to the mix.

"Roy invited me, remember?"

"Roy is supposed to be here with Suzy."

"He is."

"Then what are—"

"He didn't *un*invite me. He just added her."

"You know that's not what he meant, you—"

"Now now, name-calling is not becoming. Didn't your mother tell you that? Besides, I had no idea you'd have the nerve to show up, and there are a lot of cute Roy-type clones running around."

"But not a single brother in sight."

Please God, don't let that be Teri's voice.

"This isn't exactly the easiest crowd for me to blend in

with," Teri complained, coming around and giving Sam a high five. "Especially considering it's a family reunion."

"You can be my date," Leigh Ann declared.

"Yeah, that should make me acceptable." Teri rolled her eyes. "See why I can't trust this woman out alone?"

Jennifer's first instincts were right. She should have stayed home. "Have either of you seen Lisa?"

"She's down near the boathouse having a heart-to-heart with Benny," Teri said.

"Benny's here, too?" Jennifer asked.

"It's either him or Babs in drag," Leigh Ann threw in.

"What are they talking about?"

"Oh, like I could get within ten feet of them without looking suspicious," Teri growled. "But he did have his arm around her, and she looks like she's been crying. Of course if I had Benny's arm around me, I'd be crying, too."

"Why would she be crying?" Jennifer asked.

"The woman recently lost her husband. Cut her some slack," Leigh Ann said.

"Just murdered her husband, you mean," Jennifer pointed out.

"Miss Marsh," a girl called out.

Jennifer looked up to see Roy and Suzy, who was waving frantically, among the group getting off the pontoon boat at the dock. Suzy was in a halter top and shorts. She looked cute and even younger than she really was. She headed toward them, holding hands with Roy and towing him behind her. She'd almost reached them when she caught sight of Leigh Ann and stopped short.

"You two, go mingle," Jennifer ordered Leigh Ann and Teri.

Suzy waited until they were well out of the way before

approaching, her smile returning. She pulled Roy's arm around in front of her and nestled into his chest. Then she draped her left hand across his upper arm so Jennifer couldn't miss the sparkle of the diamond on her ring finger.

"Congratulations," Jennifer told them, smiling in spite of herself. Suzy and Roy might be one of the most unlikely couples she'd ever met, but Suzy's outright adoration and Roy's quiet affection were a more solid foundation than a lot of pairings.

Roy stared at Jennifer stonily and then withdrew his arm. He took Suzy by the shoulders. "I don't know why you'd think you'd be welcome here, considering the accusations you've been making about Lisa."

"Actually, I was invited by your aunt Melissa."

Roy looked puzzled. "Melissa? She asked you here?"

Jennifer bobbed her chin up and down. "We're here to enjoy the day. Put away any differences we might have had."

"And who's this?" Suzy gushed at Sam. "He your man?"

"Absolutely," Sam confirmed, hugging Jennifer to him.

"He's cute," Suzy observed, wiggling away from Roy and taking Jennifer's hands. "Let's let the boys talk. I want to introduce you to somebody."

She pulled Jennifer away, back toward the pavilion.

Jennifer leaned in and whispered as they walked. "You had me worried last night. Did Lisa catch you calling me?"

"No. It wasn't even her. It was Gus, and he wouldn't say anything. So I was fine, but I figured I'd had about all the spying I could manage for one day. But let's not talk about that. Your boyfriend is so hot," Suzy gushed. "Must be serious if you brought him here, huh?"

Jennifer smiled. Suzy could draw whatever conclusions she wanted to. She already knew more of the truth than was good for her.

Suzy tugged her toward an older woman unwrapping paper plates and napkins at the start of the buffet line. Her hair was dyed an unnatural black, and although age had diminished her stature, she had that same round build of the Mayfields and an obvious energy.

Suzy tapped her on the back, and the older woman looked up. "Lands, child. You gave me a start. Where's my favorite grandchild?"

"He's visiting. Grandma Dorothy, I want you to meet my friend Jennifer. She's from Macon, too."

"Is she now? Well, I'm proud to make your acquaintance. I don't mean to be rude, but I have to get everything ready, so why don't we chat while we work? Melissa is usually in charge, but she's laid up with that sprained toe of hers. Just grab the lids off the containers, set them down under them, stuff in a spoon, and we'll have it done in no time. We won't bother with the desserts until later."

Two red-cheeked boys, about eight years old, snuck up and ducked under each of Dorothy's arms. The smaller one reached out and stuck a finger in some kind of Jell-O mixture and was about to bring it to his lips when Dorothy smacked his hand. She grabbed a napkin and wiped it off.

"You two young-uns know better than that. You should be playing ball with the other kids. I hope they're not getting too close to the cars. We sure don't need any cracked windows. Suzy, get that tin of gingersnaps over on the dessert table and give them each one and only one. That will have to hold you until it's time to eat. Now off with you!"

The boys scampered after Suzy.

"Isn't she the cutest young-un?"

Jennifer nodded.

"You come over with Roy and Suzy?"

Jennifer shook her head as she wrestled with the lid of a particularly stubborn jar of pickles. "Actually, Melissa invited me. I know several members of the family. Lisa Walker—"

"Here. Let me get that." Dorothy took the jar and gave it a twist. It opened easily.

"That poor child." Dorothy stopped and stared at Jennifer. "Do you know she hasn't stopped crying since her husband was murdered?"

"Are you talking about Lisa?" Jennifer had noticed a tear here and there, but would Lisa be so clever as to keep up the front even around her family?

Dorothy nodded. "She adored that man. And I suppose he was all right to her. I didn't think it would last, but what do I know?" She shrugged her shoulders. "Melissa warned her against it from the beginning, but it was what she wanted, poor thing. When your young-uns are bent on somethin', you can't do much about it except to step in and pick up the pieces when you're right or admit that they knew better than you did when you're wrong."

"What did Lisa's mother think about the marriage?"

"Her mother's been dead these twenty years. Melissa took that child in, cared for her, loved her like a daughter rather than the great niece she is. Yes, Lisa was lucky to have her. Melissa wouldn't let anything harm that child."

Chapter 32

Melissa had raised Lisa? If Jennifer had realized Lisa and Melissa were so close, she would have stayed a lot longer at the farmhouse.

"Now, would you look at that?" Dorothy stopped what she was doing and addressed a man with a plate in each hand at the end of the table. "Edward Arthur, what do you think you're doing?"

"But it's time, Aunt Dorothy."

"Has anybody said it was time? In this family we do not eat before grace, and you know it." She took the plates and put them back in the stack.

"You about ready, Dottie? It's one o'clock," a white-haired gentleman interrupted.

She nodded. "When I can't keep them out of the food, I guess it's time. You go ahead."

The man stepped out from under the shelter and took a quick survey of the crowd. "Good afternoon," the man's voice boomed, his head swiveling to include the entire group. "I thank each and every one of you for gathering with us this afternoon. We are here today to celebrate the Mayfield family tradition, which includes lots of good eating. So I'm not about to keep you waiting with a lot of words. If you will please, bow your heads.

"Our Heavenly Father, thank you for the foods we are about to receive for the nourishment of our bodies and for the many blessings you have bestowed on this loving family. In Jesus' name we pray. Amen. Now eat up. The last ones in line may miss Melissa's vegetable casserole."

"Could never happen," Dorothy whispered to Jennifer. "She brought two washtubs full."

"Is it really that good?" Jennifer asked.

"Humph. That's it, right in the center. She's been bringing that same dish to the reunion for over thirty-five years now. You'd think no one had ever tasted it before the way they carry on about it.

"Suzy," Dorothy called, motioning the girl over. "You two helped, so you get to be first." She handed them each a paper plate.

"You go ahead," Suzy urged. "I'm going to find Roy."

The line had already formed. Jennifer looked around but Sam wasn't in sight, so she started in right where she stood, taking a scoop of this, a tad of that, and a generous helping of Melissa's famous dish. Family reunions were a vegetarian's delight, and she planned to get a good meal out of this outing if nothing else.

She popped a marinated mushroom in her mouth and headed for the drink table, where she got a cup of sweet tea. Then she looked around for a place to light and remembered that she and Sam had forgotten the lawn chairs in the backseat of the car. She was about to settle for a spot on the grass when Melissa caught up with her.

"We need to talk—just you and me, dear. If you can spare a minute. Someone was telling me about a woman who might be related to us down Valdosta way. Could be a relative of your great-grandma."

This was too good to be true. If Melissa had indeed

raised Lisa, Lisa might have let something slip. And maybe she could wrangle it out of her.

"Sure. Do you want to get a plate first?" Jennifer asked.

"I'll do that and meet you on the far side of the boat house. There's a little thicket right on the water's edge. We can have a nice quiet chat there. I'll see you in as many minutes as it takes to get my food."

If only Lisa had confided in Melissa, this case could be over this afternoon.

Jennifer made her way through the crowd and over to the boat house. She smiled at two women coming out. She heard one mention something about a water moccasin, and then the other hollered at a small girl throwing rocks off the dock.

"You get away from there right now. That water's deep, and I have no intentions of fishing you out."

The woman rushed over and grabbed the child by the hand, scolding her all the way to the picnic area.

Jennifer knew there was a reason she didn't like lakes.

Teri and Leigh Ann found her before she could get any farther.

"Tell me how you rate that you've already got food and everybody else has to stand in a line that stretches on for a quarter mile?" Teri asked, eyeing Jennifer's plate.

Leigh Ann helped herself to one of Jennifer's marinated mushrooms.

"Why are you talking to me? You're supposed to be listening," Jennifer said.

"Told you she didn't appreciate us," Leigh Ann said. "We give up a Saturday afternoon, and she can't even be civil. I've a mind not to tell her what we found out."

Whatever it was, Jennifer doubted it was worth the price of a carrot strip, let alone the mushroom.

"You really ought to work on how you treat your friends. I actually left a spot in line to come tell you what we'd heard," Teri pointed out.

"Fine. I apologize. Now spill it."

"It's not what we heard exactly. It's more what we haven't heard," Leigh Ann explained.

"Yeah," Teri agreed. "I mean, everybody is talking about the murder, except when Lisa gets near, and then they shut up. But nobody has mentioned anything about Edgar still being in love with Emma like you told us."

"Nobody?" Jennifer asked.

"Nobody. I don't think they've heard it, which means Lisa's kept it to herself—" Leigh Ann said.

"Or—" Teri began.

"Or she didn't know about it," Jennifer finished. But she had to. It was Lisa's motive for killing Edgar. "Listen, you two go ahead and eat. I've got to be somewhere. I'll talk to you later."

The area on the far side of the boat house was deserted, and for good reason. Trees grew almost to the lake. None of the undergrowth had been cleared away, and Jennifer wondered how many species of insect made their homes there.

At the edge of the water she found a small clearing and sat down on a large root. It was nice to have a moment alone, a moment to think.

Someday Suzy and Roy would bring their children to these reunions. Happy, healthy children with bright futures. And Suzy would be the frantic mother keeping her child from getting too close to the lake.

Lisa didn't have any children to mind, and suddenly

Jennifer wondered why. Had she given up children because Edgar didn't want any? Had she done that for him?

And now that he was dead, what did she have? A restaurant? Even a chain of restaurants didn't seem adequate. But if she'd loved him that much, why had she killed him?

She had to have done it. She was the only other person there that night, wasn't she? Who else could have known how to reset the security system? And who could have known that Emma was meeting Edgar that night?

Suzy might have known. She'd overheard other conversations between Edgar and Emma. Roy could as easily have heard something. Would either of them have told Lisa? Roy and Lisa were cousins. Would he have killed for her?

So many questions.

When Melissa came, she'd simply ask her. Who would know Lisa and Roy better than she?

But in the meantime, the aroma of her food was teasing her. And it was getting cold. Maybe Melissa wouldn't mind if she started without her.

Melissa would hardly notice if she'd had a nibble here and there. She tasted the gelled sea foam salad. While nutritionally questionable, it was heavenly. The corn pudding was every bit as good as any she'd ever eaten, as were the deviled eggs, and the fruit salad. The green bean casserole would make French's french fried onions proud.

She saved Melissa's casserole for last. She took a tiny bit on her plastic fork and savored it on her tongue. It was surprisingly flavorful, with a creamy goodness the likes of which she'd never tasted except for . . . Jennifer sat straight up. It couldn't be. She scooped up a huge forkful and stuffed it into her mouth. Her taste buds must be playing tricks on her. Ignoring the vegetables, it tasted just like Edgar's Special Steak Sauce. It *was* Edgar's special steak sauce.

The blow caught her on the back of the head, just below the ear. For a moment everything went black and then spun as she pitched forward. She seemed to have lost all use of her limbs.

The second blow caught her shoulder, and then she was plunging head first into cool water. It welcomed her, soothing her, cushioning her fall, enveloping her as she sank, breathless, into total blackness.

Chapter 33

People say their lives flash before them when they face death, but Jennifer wasn't so sure. What was flashing through her mind had little to do with herself and everything to do with who killed Edgar Walker. That blow to the head must have knocked some sense into her because all the bits and pieces of the last few weeks were jarred into place. Too bad she wasn't going to live to share her revelations.

The water was dark, and she couldn't seem to remember to open her eyes. But she had to. Somehow she pried loose her lids, but which way was up? Everything was spinning, spinning as if she were caught in an eddy that was sucking her farther and farther down as it drew the last bits of breath from her lungs. She was choking, choking on water, and then the blackness that was outside seemed to be inside. She said a little prayer for Emma and one for Jaimie. She lost consciousness before she finished one for herself.

She was gagging and fighting for air, desperately trying to fill her lungs. Someone cradled the back of her neck and gently turned her head as water spilled from her throat.

"It's all right," a woman's voice soothed. "You're going to be all right."

"She's breathing," the voice told someone else.

Suddenly, Jennifer choked and retched violently. Then she felt her useless body being tugged backward, and she was again on her back. A soothing cloth dabbed at her face and neck, wiping the hair from her forehead.

"Just breathe normally. Damn it. Help me get this thing off of her."

And then there was a pulling and tugging and what had lain tangled around her neck was free.

Her back hurt. So did her neck and everything inside her rib cage.

Whatever she was lying on was hard and rocky and had scraped her skin. Solid ground. Thank God.

Slowly, her eyelids parted. Wet, tangled, unnaturally blond hair brushed her cheeks. She blinked twice as the face, so close to her own, finally came into focus.

Lisa smiled. She looked surprisingly pleasant. "She's okay. She's back with us," she said, her white mesh bathing suit dripping water down Jennifer's neck.

"What?" Jennifer managed to ask. Pain caught in the back of her head and she winced. Her eyes rolled up. All she could see were treetops. She must be in the clearing where she'd sat down to eat.

"Don't try to talk. Benny, go call the paramedics."

Jennifer licked her lips. Her mouth tasted sour. "How did you—"

"I told you not to talk." Lisa laid a towel across Jennifer's chest. "I went around the side of the boat house to get some rope. I thought I heard a splash, but that damn motorboat was making so much noise I couldn't be sure. Then I saw some fabric—that shift you had on over your suit—floating on the water a few yards from the shore, and I realized someone had fallen in. I dove in after you. You're going to be fine."

Jennifer grabbed Lisa's forearm. "I know you didn't kill Edgar."

"Of course I didn't. I told you that. Now rest."

But she couldn't rest. She knew who had killed Edgar and who had tried to kill her. Emma's trial was barreling to a conclusion, and it had to be stopped before another day, another hour, passed with Emma accused of murder.

She tried to rise up, but Lisa shoved her back down.

"I'm a certified lifeguard, at least I used to be. You're to stay put."

"But you don't understand. I know."

"Know what, dear?" another woman's voice asked.

Lisa drew back and Melissa bent forward.

Jennifer shrieked with every bit of energy she could muster, but only a squeak came out.

"Why don't you make sure Benny called those paramedics," Melissa told Lisa.

Jennifer clutched at Lisa, but she was pulling away.

"I'll be right back. Melissa will take good care of you."

And then it was just the two of them—Jennifer and Melissa.

She felt her forearms wedged down as Melissa straddled her, and a hand came down over her mouth and pinched her nostrils shut. "Relax, dear, like Lisa said. This won't take long."

Melissa was right. It wouldn't take long, in her weakened state, for her to pass out again. She had to do something, but what? Melissa's weight was resting on her torso. Jennifer's hands were free and so were her legs, but they weren't any good to her with her arms and body pinned to the ground.

Her breath was leaving again, but she hadn't come out of the darkness to be plunged back into it. There had to be something she could do. Something . . . And then she remembered an old childhood trick she used to play when someone had a hand over her mouth. She forced her tongue between her lips and licked the inside of Melissa's hand.

Melissa jerked back, and the weight on Jennifer's forearms eased just enough. As Jennifer gasped for air, she mustered every ounce of strength in her body and twisted to her right, knocking Melissa on her side. She didn't have to win, she told herself. All she had to do was delay. She rolled onto her face and into a ball like a turtle drawing in all its appendages. She felt Melissa grab at her back, trying to push her over. At least if Melissa killed her now, she'd have to leave marks, and there'd be no pretense of drowning.

"What the heck?" It was Sam's voice. He pushed past Melissa, turned Jennifer over, and cradled her to him.

Lisa was right behind him, covering her with a blanket.

Jennifer coughed and drew in precious air. "It was Melissa." Jennifer strained against his embrace. "She doesn't have arthritis. She's strong as a horse. She killed Edgar, and she was trying to kill me."

Chapter 34

Jennifer liked being pampered. Having Sam at her beck and call was something she could get used to. He was a pretty darned good cook even if he had a philosophical problem with leaving the ham out of a grilled ham and cheese. But that was all right. He was learning.

She stretched her feet against the far side of the sofa. Muffy stirred and gave Jennifer's hand another lick. The dog had been so upset when Sam came to feed and walk her last night while she was at the hospital that he'd stayed the night. He'd even let her sleep on the foot of the bed. They both knew better.

She was fine. Really she was. The doctor had kept her overnight for observation. All she needed was a few days of relaxation.

On the coffee table was the large vase of cut flowers that Monique, April, Teri, and Leigh Ann had sent. She had scared them silly. At the lake was the first time she'd ever seen Teri cry.

Being loved was good. Being alive and loved was even better.

Sam brought in a lunch tray with her grilled cheese sandwich and a bowl of steaming tomato soup. He set it on her lap and made a big production of tucking a paper napkin under her chin. "Your coordination may not be quite back to normal," he told her, kissing her nose.

Then he collapsed into the armchair.

"Aren't you having any?" she asked.

"Maybe later. I enjoy watching you eat."

Good. She enjoyed watching him cook. "What have you heard from the police?"

"They arrested Melissa for the assault on you right after we left in the ambulance. She's admitted to that much."

"But why'd she do it?"

"You kept insisting to anyone who would listen that Lisa had killed Edgar. She wasn't about to let Lisa be charged with anything."

"I guess not." She took a sip of soup. "This is really good, by the way."

She wiped the corner of her mouth. It wasn't easy trying to eat with her legs stretched straight out in front of her. "When I found out Lisa and Melissa were like mother and daughter, and then I tasted her vegetable casserole and realized the steak sauce was her recipe, everything fell into place—right about the time *I* fell into the water."

She rose up and Sam was immediately on his feet, stuffing a pillow behind her back. "Thanks. It all suddenly made sense. Roy must have overheard Edgar setting up the meeting with Emma the night he died. He probably knew about some of the earlier meetings as well. Suzy had figured out Edgar was in love with Emma, so I'm sure Roy must have suspected, too. And Melissa was the only one he was likely to have told. He wouldn't have wanted to hurt Lisa by telling her."

"One thing that bothered me from the beginning," Sam said, "was the security system."

Jennifer nodded. "That's one of the reasons I was

convinced Lisa was the murderer. But surely during the years Lisa was married to Edgar, Melissa would have been told about the codes, especially with the two of them working odd hours at the restaurant. She could let herself in the gate without anyone knowing, kill Edgar, push his body into the pool, attack Emma, let herself into the house, turn the pool alarm back on, and get herself off the property without anyone knowing it."

"And before you arrived several hours later. But how could she have done all that if she was crippled with arthritis and a sprained toe?"

"She wasn't. I told you that at the lake," Jennifer explained. "The arthritis must have been an act for my benefit. I showed up shortly after Edgar's death, and she was suspicious. When she invited me to the picnic to stage my seemingly accidental death, she put on the sprained toe act, so the family wouldn't question why she was using a cane."

Jennifer broke off a small piece of sandwich and fed it to Muffy. The dog wouldn't leave her long enough to eat her own food. "In her mind, Melissa was just protecting her own. Lisa and Roy had built up that restaurant with Melissa's recipe and her blessings, and Edgar was using that success to lure Emma back to him."

"And the prenup meant he could steal the restaurant and the franchise business right out from under Lisa," Sam said.

"Right," she agreed. "It was Melissa who was getting that ten percent of the gross receipts, and she would still get it, but Lisa would be out in the cold. Lisa had as much invested in that restaurant as Edgar did."

"Well, now she's got his share, and it looks as if she and Emma can go forward with the franchise."

A knock sounded on the door, and Sam rose to open it. Mrs. Walker rushed past him to Jennifer. "Oh dear, oh dear, oh dear. Just look at you. You look like death itself. But at least you're being fed."

Jennifer screwed up her face. No wonder Sam had insisted he couldn't find a mirror when she'd fixed her hair.

"I'm fine," Jennifer assured her, "regardless of what I look like. What are you doing here?"

"I had to see for myself that you were all right. I made Walter bring me over."

A sharp pain shot through her head as Jennifer twisted to see Ornsby standing by the door. He was holding a vase filled with at least a dozen roses.

"Did he tell you about Allison?" Jennifer asked.

"Yes, and I'm quite put out about it. He should never have kept her existence from me. I always wanted children, you see. She should have been part of our lives— Edgar's and mine. I do so hope she's fond of dogs. She and I have got to get to work on this franchise plan. Lisa, too, of course. We've put off our investors far too long as it is."

"How is Lisa?"

"She's holding up pretty well, now that the initial shock of learning that Melissa killed Edgar is wearing off. She's had quite a blow. First losing her husband, and now effectively losing her foster mother."

"She's got Benny," Sam threw in.

"True, but they're just friends," Mrs. Walker insisted. "I hardly think he could keep up with her. She's quite a dynamo, you know."

"Does that mean the charges against you—" Jennifer began.

"Heckemyer is filing a motion for dismissal Monday morning," Ornsby said, bringing the flowers over and setting them next to the other bouquet.

"You didn't have to—" Jennifer started.

"We didn't," Mrs. Walker interrupted. "I was so flustered over what happened to you, flowers hadn't yet entered my mind. We met the delivery man outside the door."

"Sam?" Jennifer smiled.

He fished the card from among the blooms. "Wish I could take credit for this one, but I've been pretty busy."

He opened the small envelope, pulled out the card, and read. " 'Jen, remember your promise. Front page exclusive. You get one day of rest. I'll see you early Monday morning. Love, Teague.' "

Sam glared at her. "Love, Teague? Exclusive?"

She'd known that deal with the devil would come back to haunt her, but she'd given her word. She'd have to go through with it.

Jennifer stuffed the last bit of sandwich in her mouth and gulped it down. She might not be getting any more of Sam's cooking for a while.

"What were you thinking?" he demanded.

"If I hadn't promised him, we would never have found out that Allison was Natalie."

He wasn't saying a word. She liked it better when he yelled.

"I almost drowned. Have you forgotten?"

"No, and you're fine. You told me so yourself."

"I don't think I'm as fine as I thought. As a matter of fact, I think I'm having a relapse." She burrowed down into the sofa cushions and let out a phony-sounding cough.

"You can't have a relapse from drowning," Sam pointed out.

"But I could catch pneumonia."

"Children, please," Mrs. Walker commanded. "Be thankful you still have one another. At a time like this, everything else fades to nothing."

Sam knelt down next to the couch and drew Jennifer to him. And, for a moment at least, all else did fade to nothing.

Chapter 35

Every nerve in Maxie's body stood alert. She could sense danger like a mouse could sense a cat. But she continued to stare into the lake. If she moved too soon, she'd give herself away.

Then she tucked and rolled, just as the cane came whizzing over her head. She lunged back, jerking the wood from Missy Burdette's hands, caught her with an uppercut, and brought a blow down on the back of her neck. Burdette crumpled to the ground like a wet dishrag.

"It's all over, Missy," Maxie told her. "I know you killed Rufus Donaldson, even if you'd only meant to confront him that night at his factory. He took your recipe for Rocky Road fudge and built an empire with it. Then he planned to toss your niece away like yesterday's newspaper, without so much as alimony. But it didn't work, Missy. Murder is an easy answer. It's never the right answer."

"What's going on here?" Oscar Mobley's gruff voice called as he tramped through the woods. She'd called him before going down to the water by herself. Maxie was no fool.

"She's all yours," Maxie declared. "Missy Burdette murdered Donaldson."

"Well, I'll be, Maxie. Guess I owe you a major apology.

You ever think of becoming part of the force? We could use someone like you."

Maxie grinned. She'd finally won his respect. And while she was content to be a private investigator, it sure was nice to be asked.

And it sure would be nice to be published.

Jennifer let out a huge sigh and typed THE END at the bottom of the page.

"So what do you think, Muff? Is the truth buried deep enough that no one would connect Maxie's adventure with Edgar Walker's murder?"

Muffy shook all over and then collapsed on the floor. Jennifer took that as doggy for no.

She'd never get away with it. She might as well dump the whole file.

She stared at the delete button, but she couldn't quite make herself do it. Maybe there was something in there, some scene, some character, something she could salvage for another book.

She pressed the save button and pulled up a new document.

A blank page. The first page of a new novel. It stared back at her, taunting her. No matter how many books she wrote, starting one never got any easier.

She closed her eyes and let her mind go. Then her fingers found the keys.

Serena Callas looked like a cross between a superhero and a biker chick, but she was one of Atlanta's most prominent private eyes. Her bleached hair flew about her face like a flag flapping in a good wind as she tugged down the black leather of her vest and jerked open the door of her Jag. A small tattoo of a wasp showed on her upper thigh

*just below her miniskirt as she climbed in and slammed
the door behind her. Her lips formed into a pout.*

    Murder was her business.

    "Yes," Jennifer purred. "Now that's more like it."

Wish you had another
Jennifer Marsh mystery to read?

Why not go back to where it all began?

DYING TO GET PUBLISHED

The First Jennifer Marsh Mystery

by Judy Fitzwater

"*Dying to Get Published* will entertain all writers. . . .
[It] offers a word to the wise: Never thwart a mystery
writer, published or unpublished."
—CAROLYN G. HART

DYING TO GET PUBLISHED

The First Jennifer Marsh Mystery

by Judy Fitzwater

Aspiring murder-mystery novelist Jennifer Marsh didn't let a few rejection letters stop her. Instead she concocted a killer scheme for her next novel.

Contains an exclusive interview with first-time novelist Judy Fitzwater.

Published by Fawcett Crest Books.
Available at your local bookstore.